THE KEYS OF MY PRISON

RICOCHET TITLES

The Crime on Cote des Neiges by David Montrose

Murder Over Dorval by David Montrose

The Body on Mount Royal by David Montrose

Sugar-Puss on Dorchester Street by Al Palmer

The Long November by James Benson Nablo

Waste No Tears by Hugh Garner

The Mayor of Côte St. Paul by Ronald J. Cooke

Hot Freeze by Douglas Sanderson

Blondes are My Trouble by Douglas Sanderson

Gambling with Fire by David Montrose

The Keys of My Prison by Frances Shelley Wees

THE KEYS OF MY PRISON

FRANCES SHELLEY WEES

A
Ricochet
Book

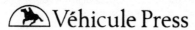

Véhicule Press

Published with the assistance of the Canada Council for the Arts and the Canada Book Fund of the Department of Canadian Heritage.

Funded by the Government of Canada
Financé par le gouvernement du Canada | **Canadä**

Series editor: Brian Busby
Adaptation of original cover: J.W. Stewart
Special assistance: Geri Newell
Typeset in Minion by Simon Garamond
Printed by Marquis Printing Inc.

LIBRARY AND ARCHIVES CANADA CATALOGUING IN PUBLICATION

Wees, Frances Shelley, 1902-1982, author
The keys of my prison / Frances Shelley Wees ;
introduction by Rosemary Aubert.

(Ricochet books)
Issued in print and electronic formats.
ISBN 978-1-55065-453-0 (paperback).– ISBN 978-1-55065-459-2
(epub)

I. Aubert, Rosemary, writer of introduction II. Title.
III. Series: Ricochet books

PS8545.E38K4 2016   C813'.54   C2016-902057-6

C2016-902058-4

Published by Véhicule Press, Montréal, Québec, Canada
www.vehiculepress.com

Distribution in Canada by LitDistCo
www.litdistco.ca

Distributed in the U.S. by Independent Publishers Group
www.ipgbook.com

Printed in Canada on FSC certified paper

INTRODUCTION

Rosemary Aubert

The Keys of My Prison is a terrifying and original take on the story of Dr. Jekyll and Mr. Hyde. The present edition gives the reader an edge-of-the seat experience that hasn't been available for fifty years. Time has not diminished the suspense. Nor has it dulled the emotional involvement the reader feels in this powerful story of ordinary life gone suddenly and horribly wrong.

When the 1966 reissue of this 1956 book was published, it was billed as "A Gothic Novel of Suspense." These were the days when Alfred Hitchcock reigned supreme, and most significantly, the days long before two advances that could have shot this story out of the water: the Internet and DNA testing.

But they were absent back then. So a woman whose husband opens his eyes and sees her and asks, "Who the hell are you?" doesn't have a lot to fall back on.

Up to that moment, Julie Jonason had every reason to believe that she has been married to the perfect man. Not only is he handsome, kind, industrious and patient, he has done what Julie believed no man would ever do: marry her despite an ugly black birth mark obscuring a great deal of her face.

Medical science solves that problem as time goes by, allowing Julie to believe that she now has everything: an ancestral home in one of Toronto's most elegant and expensive neighbourhoods, an inheritance from a devoted— and extremely rich—father, a lifestyle of ease and luxury, a sweet child—and best of all—a perfect husband: Rafe, wonderful Rafe.

But when he is injured in a car accident and awakes after a prolonged period in a coma, Julie slowly realizes that the life she had known is gone. Mercifully, the accident has spared his gorgeous body. But it has totally altered his personality. He is now gruff, vulgar, dismissive of Julie and totally ignorant of his role as a father. He drinks. He seems to care nothing for the home he once shared with his wife, his son, his devoted aunt and the friends of the family who have supported and encouraged him since he was young, inexperienced and uncouth—but never bitter and mean as he is now.

He seems to have completely forgotten Julie's late father, a powerful man whose faith helped him to become powerful, too and who turned over his beloved daughter with happiness and hope. Happiness now forgotten and hope abandoned by Julie, if not by a few stalwart supporters who, unlike her, persist in believing that this *is* Rafe and that he will "come around".

The "case" progresses through the work of two detectives called into service by a friend of Julie's. The two are vaguely reminiscent of Holmes and Watson. Jonathan Merrill, the chief investigator is a lean, quiet man, a psychologist of few words but great logical powers. His sidekick, the undercover police officer Henry Lake, unlike Watson, is an active participant in solving the mystery. He is particularly skilled at playing the Jonasons' butler. His impersonation is without flaw and his ability to gather information a valuable help in finally figuring out what is going on here. It also helps that the two have fingerprint and dental evidence to back their theories about the mystery.

Like all gripping psychological thrillers, this book depends on giving with one hand, then taking away with the other. Every time Julie feels that she might be leading "her" Rafe toward healing, he takes a fresh step back into the dark depths of his "other" personality, leaving Julie teetering between elation and despair.

With the combination of logic and footwork, the answer to this strange puzzle is gradually revealed. And in the moment of final understanding, this remarkable story changes from a profoundly unsettling gothic novel to a classic murder mystery of the greatest cunning.

Like its hero, this book has been asleep for a long time. But now it is awake again and ready to frighten a whole new set of readers.

Frances Shelley Wees (née Johnson) was born in Oregon in 1902 and came to Canada at an early age, going on to live in Alberta, Saskatchewan and—for the most part—Ontario. She spent seventeen years in Toronto, which would account for her evocative and accurate portrayal of the city in this book.

Wees was the tireless author of two dozen mystery and romance novels, among them the mystery *Lost* House, the second book Harlequin ever published, as well as articles, poems, serial pieces and readers for schoolchildren. She once told an aspiring writer that she had sometimes had to mend socks with one hand and type manuscripts with the other. A teacher, Wees was deeply devoted to all aspects of her busy life, including a dedication to the Chatauqua movement. The author spent her final days in British Columbia, dying there in 1982.

Rosemary Aubert is the award-winning author of the Ellis Portal mystery series. Her work is based on her experience as a criminologist. She lives in Toronto.

*Mee thinkes I have the keyes of my prison in mine
own hand, and no remedy presents it selfe so soon to
my heart, as mine own sword.*

JOHN DONNE

CHAPTER ONE

As she rested on the cushioned chaise longue in the window corner of the hospital room, Julie heard Rafe stir and again begin to mutter. She got up quickly and went to his bed, to look down at him and to set her palm gently along his cheek. His face felt cool, almost normal; the swelling was nearly gone and the dark softness of the bruise was turning into firm clear flesh. There was still a bandage above his forehead, but, Dr. Prescott had assured Julie, the small fracture was healed. Concussion had kept Rafe insensible. It was almost two weeks since the accident, and for the first five days of that time he had been motionless and silent, so that to look at him was to look at death and to feel it, cold and gloating, in her despairing heart. Now the danger was past and Rafe was truly getting better. For a week he had been trying to talk, even making sentences now and then. They were confusing groups of words, those sentences, somehow queerly unfamiliar to Julie. Although they appeared to have some deep meaning to Rafe, who struggled so hard to say them, they made no sense to her.

Her hand, with the gleaming diamonds on its wedding finger, was just the familiar length of his cheek. She lifted it and allowed herself the luxury of tracing the lines of his lips gently with the tips of her fingers. He had been so desperately far away, so lost and so remote, and now he was coming back. He was still deeply unconscious—knowing nothing, Dr. Prescott said—but his mind was troubled. Julie had found herself for days now puzzled and even a little frightened at the dark mystery of the human mind. Rafe's face was full of strain when he tried to talk, as if he made some strong effort in his hidden thinking. His mouth, so beautifully chiseled, held no relaxation; the lips were taut under her caressing fingers. His eyes, shut tight, held tension in the lids. It was as if he were struggling to come back from a far country, a strange country which Julie did not know, a place at the other side of nowhere, in which he had lived for all these long days since the accident.

The lips moved, and Julie took her hand away quickly. He began to speak again, and his voice was harsh, an odd bitter harshness in a voice that had always been gentle. He mouthed a long string of indistinguishable words and tried to turn his head on the pillow. Julie moved back so that she was not touching him, so that she did not disturb the blanket over him.

He said clearly, "Not much of a wedding ring."

Something warm happened in Julie's heart, as if the sun had struck a bud and a flower had opened. Not much of a wedding ring! She let her eyes rest on the narrow band of solid, square-cut diamonds, each one perfect, chosen to be perfect just for her, Julie Macrae, who had never dared to dream of perfection. It was the most lovely wedding ring in the world, so lovely that she often did not wear her engagement ring, which was a beautiful stone. But the engagement ring had never seemed real or believable; the wedding ring was true, and had meant something beyond all her hopes. It was real, and it was hers, and Rafe had chosen it and put it on her finger; and in every moment of their life together he had more than lived up to the promises he had made her with the ring.

And now he was thinking of her. Lying there lost and alone in a black mist, his mind was groping for her, for their wedding day, years ago, for their beginning love together.

Not much of a wedding ring!

A swish of sound came abruptly into the room as the door opened and the noises of the busy hospital corridor broke into the silence. They faded again as the heavy door swung silently shut on its airlock.

The day nurse, Miss Burnell, came to the other side of Rafe's bed. She gave Julie a brief glance, slipped a thermometer into Rafe's mouth expertly, and set her fingers on his pulse. She glanced at her watch. Then her eyes came to Julie and went over her, in a cool measuring look. Absorbed in counting pulse-beats, she forgot to cover that inner self of hers, the curious, envious, insecure self that was so obvious in spite of the certainty of her bearing, the crispness of her uniform, the brassy smooth perfection of her dark-blonde hair, so smooth that it looked beaten on her head instead of brushed. She was not a very generous person, not very pleasant, not very real, but she was a wonderful nurse. "Couldn't find a better for an unconscious man," Dr. Prescott had told Julie with one of his wry grins. "We'll take her off when Rafe comes to."

She laid Rafe's wrist down again on the white seersucker spread and then smiled at Julie. "He's doing just fine. His pulse is normal." She took off her watch and dropped it into her pocket. She pushed her cuffs up a little. "You look pretty beat up, Mrs. Jonason. You need about a two-day sleep. Nobody can do twenty-four-hour duty for a couple of weeks and stay on deck."

"I've slept quite a lot."

"Well, that *is* a pretty good couch," Miss Burnell conceded, whipping the thermometer from Rafe's mouth. She looked at it. "I've spent quite a few hours of my life on it, too. Dr. Prescott likes this corner room—it's the nicest one on the floor—and I work for Dr. Prescott most of the time and he usually wants me on nights in the beginning of a bad case. I sit on that couch with my feet up and knit." She looked at the thermometer. "One sure thing, it's easier on the feet than dancing."

"What is his temperature?"

Miss Burnell gave her a sharp glance. "Only one degree.

He's certainly out of the woods. Why don't you go home and take a couple of sleeping pills and get rested up? About tomorrow night he's going to come out of this and you'll want to look bright and fresh."

"You think it will be so long?"

"Well, I'm not the doctor, although I've certainly seen plenty of these cases. Nobody can tell what they're going to do. I had a notion this morning, when I first came on duty, that he was already just about out of it. He opened his eyes and looked straight at me and said my name."

"Said your name!"

"Well, I don't think he really knew me." Miss Burnell went into the little washroom and ran water over the thermometer. She came back slipping it into its case. "He called me Bess. That's not really my name. My name is Betty. He looked straight at me and said 'Bess, Bess!' I got quite a start, because my brother-in-law—that's my sister's husband— he always called me Bess, and I kind of liked it. He says my hair is the color of Queen Elizabeth's ... you know, the first one, the old girl away back when. Not that I'd know, but he read a book once, or something."

Julie said slowly, "But my husband doesn't know you. He's never seen you."

The nurse looked down at Rafe's face, quiet now, as if he were really asleep and his mind at rest. "No, he's never seen me. I've never seen him, anyway. I'd have remembered. He must be terribly handsome, when there aren't bruises and bandages. I always notice those tall, blond, handsome men. There aren't enough of them. So I know I've never seen him, and of course he wouldn't know that my name was Betty. But it seemed for a minute that he was looking right at me and knowing what he said." She put a hand to the shining cap of her hair. "Maybe he knows somebody else named Bess who's got hair like mine. That kind of thing happens."

"He doesn't know anybody named Bess. He never has."

Miss Burnell's eyes were suddenly amused and then her lids dropped. "No, I'm sure he doesn't," she said. "It's just one of those things." She straightened Rafe's bed expertly while Julie stood watching her. "It's five to four," she said busily. "Miss Parker's coming on now. Would you like a cup of tea? I'll make up a tray and she can bring it in to you."

CHAPTER TWO

JULIE PAID THE TAXI DRIVER and went up the walk to the white-painted door of her own big stone house. The leaves of the maples, standing guard at the side of the walk, were drifting down over the lawn, giving it an untidy look as the yellow and brown and bronzed red piled up on the grass, still green with the October rains. Julie picked up a huge perfect leaf and carried it into the house with her, looking at it absently.

The door was unlocked and the wide front hall warm and welcoming, with a small fire leaping and dancing in the fireplace at the end under the curving stair. It touched the keys of her beloved mahogany Bechstein, and the very sight of them comforted her. Her father had built this house, and in places it had a baronial touch—in this hall, for instance, big enough for fireplace, settee, grand piano, and wide curving stair, which he had very likely copied from some big house he had glimpsed in Scotland, and Hugh Macrae had decided early not to be poor; so that his clear blue eye had taken note of everything that looked rich and warm. Not for him the porridge and blue milk for breakfast, nor the shivering chill of a damp wind creeping through meager garments. He hadn't wanted poverty and misery and discomfort for anyone, having known it so well himself, and perhaps that had been the secret of his great success. When he moved up he took everyone with him, down to the last small errand boy. The success of Hugh Macrae had been everyone's success, and everyone knew it and had wanted to help. He had died too soon— for himself, for everyone.

Julie's mind had been on her father all the way home

from the hospital, on her father and on the liking he had had for Rafe, his real love for Rafe, and the trust and confidence that had lain between the two from their first meeting. Somehow her mind kept clinging to the memory, being warmed by it.

Pulling off her gloves, with the big maple leaf and her alligator bag tucked under her arm, she turned into the living room at the right of the hall. Edith was there, Edith Macrae, her father's sister, sitting stiffly upright as always in her favorite wing chair under a lamp beside the fireplace, working away vigorously at a needlepoint chair seat, her cheeks pink, her fluffy white hair curling all over her head, her glasses pushed well down on the end of her nose. It was a comforting picture. Something inside Julie relaxed a little.

She said gently, "I'm home, Edie."

Her aunt looked up, startled, and then put the needlepoint down with a quick movement on the table beside her chair. She got up, pushed her glasses into place, and came across the floor, her eyes searching Julie's face. "I didn't hear you, child," she said. "How is it, dear? How is Rafe? Is he better, then?"

"Much better. His pulse is normal and his temperature almost normal. And now they've given him a sedative— he was restless, talking and trying to make some kind of sense. It seems queer to give him a sedative when he's been asleep so long. But we have to remember he isn't asleep, Dr. Prescott explained, he's bothering and worrying about something ... maybe the accident. He'll be blaming himself somehow, even if it wasn't his fault. So he's quiet and asleep, and they sent me home. He'll sleep all night."

Edie's hands were busy with the amber button at the neck of Julie's coat. "Did they give you something to take too? You could do with a night's sleep."

Julie dropped down on the sofa just inside the door and leaned her head back. "I think I might be able to sleep for about ten hours without it. It's so wonderful to have him getting well. It's so wonderful."

"Yes," Edie said bluntly. She bustled out to the hall and hung the coat in the cupboard. She came back and sat down on the sofa beside Julie. "I've been praying, over the stitches," she said. "I gave the Lord a piece of my mind, too. I said to Him, look here, this has gone on long enough. It isn't as if You had to punish that boy for anything, or Julie either. He's been a good boy, and she's been a good girl and she's had enough to bear. I think it's time You took off the pressure." She twisted down the corners of her mouth. "Sometimes I think even the Lord needs a woman to remind him about details. All men are kittle cattle when it comes to details." She put out a hand and touched Julie's black hair. "Those curls need washing and a good brushing, and you need a hot bath with plenty of scent in it, and then I'll rub your back. What've you had to eat?"

"I had a tray at the hospital. I don't know, exactly."

"Sawdust with white sauce, no doubt."

"How's my baby, Edie? I suppose he's asleep."

"He's a dear, dear boy." Edie got to her feet. "I'll bring you a cup of tea, dear, and some cold chicken. We're having a time to use up that Sunday fowl. I've not much appetite either, and Nellie and Jennie are both moping. I should've known better than to have a big chicken for dinner yesterday. But things'll improve now." She moved toward the door. "Little Hughie reached for his spoon tonight. It's much too soon, when he's only fourteen months, but he did. He'll be feeding himself like a man before we know it. His daddy will hardly know him, not seeing him for so long."

Julie straightened the alligator purse carefully on the couch beside her and laid the gloves evenly upon it. She picked up the leaf again and sat looking at it, at the thin, perfect fabric, the careful intricacy of the veining, the beginning transparency of the color. Her eyes saw it, but her mind did not. She put it down finally and got up to walk across the floor to the fire, to stand with a hand on the white-painted mantel and stare into the flames. She put the other hand down to smooth the pleats in her dark green skirt, and the firelight caught in the diamonds of her ring. She turned the ring slowly with her thumb, regarding the small flickering glints of changing color.

Edie came in with a round silver tray, with the teapot on it covered with the white embroidered cozy, two of the best pink-flowered cups, and a plate of thin sandwiches. Her blue eyes, paler than Julie's own but still very blue, came to Julie's face again. They flicked away quickly. She set the tray down on a low table and drew up a chair. "Come on then," she said firmly. She sat down herself and poured out the steaming, fragrant liquid.

Julie sat on the hassock and lifted her cup obediently. The room was full of silence; only the gentle whisper of the flames and the slow ponderous ticking of the tall clock in the hall broke the soft quiet.

"Edie."

"Yes, Juliet?"

"It's Rafe."

"Yes."

"I know he's getting well. Anybody can see that. He was so white and still, so deathly … and his face was so bruised, so swollen … and his heart scarcely beat at all, and then he had such a high temperature … all that is gone."

"Yes."

The clock in the hall grumbled and cleared its throat. It struck eight in a hoarse, old-man's voice, protesting but dutiful. The last stroke died away.

"Edie, Rafe has never known anyone named Bess, has he?"

Edie set her cup into its saucer and put the saucer down on the tray. She reached over and got the needlepoint, white lilies on a brilliant scarlet ground. Her small quick fingers pushed the needle in and out, in and out. She looked up.

"I never heard the name in my life. But it could be that he's known someone named Bess when he was a small boy. People's minds go back, they say, in the kind of trouble he's been having. They get a knock on the head and their minds go back, to something they've forgotten."

Julie nodded.

"He's been talking about someone named Bess?"

"You can't really call it talking. This morning he opened his eyes and the nurse thought he was speaking to her …. He said, 'Bess, Bess.'"

"Which nurse? That hard blonde creature? Nat Prescott shouldn't have put her on the case. She's a trouble maker. Why would she tell you a thing like that? Is her name Bess? She's vain, that's what she is, a peacock creature. She's jealous, Julie. I told Nat Prescott not to make you have to do with her, after the first time I laid eyes on her. Hard, she is, and as brassy as her hair."

"She's a good nurse. And she was telling the truth. Because tonight he talked about Bess again to me. He said …"

"Well?"

"Well, he said …" Julie stopped. "He said, 'Bess, look … I'm on the train already! Take a look, I'm on the train already.'"

Edie stared at Julie for a moment, and then her hands began to move on her needlepoint again. She took a long breath. "Five years old," she said. "That's what he's gone back to, a boy of five years old, playing train. It's as plain as the nose on your face."

After a long time Julie said, "I suppose that's it. And he'd been playing with a little girl named Bess. He's never mentioned her. But he never talks much about his childhood, does he?"

"It wasn't much of a childhood, traipsing around from one logging camp to another, up there in the British Columbia wilderness. But there'd have been other children.

He went to school, some of the time anyway, although Annie taught him until she died. Until he was ten." She looked up. "Annie's letters didn't mention any child named Bess, and I wouldn't've thought there was one .... She wrote so many letters and always put in everything. But maybe there was a family with a little girl named Bess happened along and didn't stay long, and Annie maybe didn't think to mention it, and when you think of it, Juliet, Rafe doesn't even remember much about Annie, about his own mother."

"No."

"He hadn't much of a childhood."

"Maybe that's it," Julie said slowly.

"Maybe what's it?"

"Maybe he was very lonely. Maybe he tried to forget all about it. Maybe that's why he has so few memories. And it's all buried, so that now when he isn't conscious the old hidden things come up to the surface. I think that makes sense." Julie got up quickly and went to the mirror over the mantel. She put up a hand to the cloud of her thick-springing black hair, to the bits curling against her neck. "It needs cutting, too," she said thoughtfully. She looked at herself calmly, at the shadows around the dark-blue eyes, at the vulnerability of her mouth. Perhaps it was terrible to love Rafe so much, to be so drowned in fear at the faintest breath of division between them. It was a selfish love; she owed him so much, she needed him so much even yet. But he wanted it so; he wanted as much to be close to her as she did to be close to him. He needed her, he clung to her; every word, every thought, every breath they had had since they had been married was shared, as if they were indeed a single being.

Edie said firmly, "He said something else, then?"

Julie turned and sat down again on the hassock. She locked her fingers around her knees.

"What was it?"

"Edie ... tell me again about his mother. Tell me the whole story all over again."

23

"Why? You know it well, my dear."

Julie shivered.

"You think he's going to be strange, when he wakes? You think there's something not just right?"

"He's so close to waking. But he hasn't said anything yet … that belongs in this world. This afternoon he spoke about my wedding ring. I thought it was mine he meant. But if it was, it's the only thing he's said about our life, about his life now. And I don't think it was *my* wedding ring. He said, 'Not much of a wedding ring,' in a queer, scornful, way." Julie stopped. "A self-accusing way," she decided, and looked at Edie quickly.

"Juliet, you are not to be fey. I won't have it."

"I'm not being fey. I'm facing the meaning in his voice. It frightened me, but I'm facing it. That's not being fey."

"Well, it's being stupid. Self-accusing, indeed! Juliet, the lad was only eighteen when he came here! He was a child. He'd lived in the woods all his life. He'd only two years of high school, and that by correspondence. He'd known very few people. He'd read few books. I don't know what you've got into your mind, but you can put it out. He's had a bad crack on the head, and a mercy he's not dead, with the car smashed to bits and him hurled out through the roof. His mind's gone back into some magazine he's read, or a thing he's heard, or something that's got no bearing on anything."

Julie took a long breath.

"As for wedding rings, it may have been Annie's ring he was speaking of, his mother's. It *wasn't* much of a wedding ring, a band of thin plain gold. I didn't see it when she was married, nobody saw it, because she ran away with her man, with Rafe's father, as you know well. But when she died they took the ring off her finger, and when Rafe came he had her few treasures in his box, and the ring came with them. I've said little about it, thinking it might make Rafe sad, but it's up in my box now. A band of thin plain gold, and well worn with the hard work she'd done, our Annie. And she loved her man and was well satisfied with him, and she wasn't one to complain in any taking, but it may be that the boy, and likely even the man his father, didn't think the ring was enough. She was a sweet thing, our Annie, small and sweet, and she gave up much for the man of her choosing."

"Yes," Julie said.

Edie got up and went back to her own chair, to pull the lamp close over her work. "Eat a sandwich, Juliet."

Julie picked one up and nibbled at it obediently. It was good.

"My brother would've let her marry him, the big blond Icelander, the man Lief Jonason. He was a good man, although he had not much English and was only a woods-man. But Annie didn't believe that Hugh would be so wise or so understanding, and she had her own mother's fears to remember. So she ran away."

Julie waited.

Edie sighed. "I told you the story so often when you were little, my dear. I told you all the stories." She took a long breath. "You don't need stories now. You've got your own life."

"It's like this," Julie said, and licked her fingers delicate-ly. Edie's eyes flicked to the tray, and Julie followed them, found the small folded napkin, and took it up. "It's like this, darling. There's something deep in Rafe's mind that I don't know anything about, and it's been troubling him. If only you could see the strain on his face and the struggle when he tries to talk! And I was sure I knew everything about him ... even all the books he'd read, even all the children he'd played with. He used to tell me stories too, remember? Before ... well, before we were married, even. Remember? So I thought I knew everything. But I don't. He's not inventing, now. Whatever he's saying comes from a place that's been real. It hurts him. It troubles him. And

25

I haven't a clue. I thought … maybe it's something that never happened to him. Maybe it's something his mother told him. You see? And I know she hadn't had a happy time when she was small, back in Scotland."

"She had a devil for a father."

"I know."

"She wouldn't have told her small lad so."

"She hasn't *seemed* to … he hasn't mentioned it. But she may have said something when he was little, not realizing what she was doing. What kind of devil?"

The pink color rose in Edie's cheeks, in two round spots. "The nasty kind. The worst kind. Arrogant, superior, selfish—oh, but I couldna tell you how selfish the man was! And we *knew*, in our house, because Annie's mother, who was my mother's cousin, had been brought up with us. And when the man came courting, my mother told her cousin—Lucy her name was, Rafe's grandmother Lucy—that the man was no good. But he was a handsome blackguard with a sweet face and soft ways, and he wooed and won her overnight, you might say, and they were married and he took her away to Glasgow. He was a Lowlander. It's true that we were poor at the time; we were only poor crofters, and he had a job in the city and elegant ways. But it soon turned out that it was Lucy who had to have a job in the city, and him and his elegant ways lived off her. It was scrubbing the floors of the rich folk that she had to do, and he worked her like a slave, and lied to her and tricked her and betrayed her always. And he didn't want children, he hated them. He was a child himself and jealous of other children. So that's when wee Annie was only six or seven, Lucy sent her back to us to raise. Annie went back to her mother and father now and then, but mostly she came up along with Hugh and me, and welcome, too. She was a dear wee thing, our Annie, but always timid; and we knew she'd seen her father knocking her mother about and heard her mother weeping in the darkness, and maybe it's a good thing the big braw Jonason, Rafe's father, swept her off her feet; because she was afraid of men, down deep in her heart, and might never have married else."

"Rafe doesn't look like his grandfather?"

"No, no. He's the spit and image of his father, as I remember well. Big and fair, with a swing to his shoulders, and a walk as if he owned the world. There's not a trace of Annie in him, even. He's all his father."

"She wouldn't have told him of her own mother. It's all too far away and long ago. She was too young when it happened, and Rafe was too young to hear it from her."

"No, but if she *had* told him ... and speaking of wedding rings ... it wasn't a wedding ring her father should have given her mother. It was a bridle, with big blinders and a steel bit, and a horsewhip along with it. He drove her with no mercy and he told her nothing but lies. He was a man for the women. All his family were ruthless and sly, and he was the worst of the lot; stole cattle and women wherever they could, but he looked down on honest crofters. He looked down on his wife till the day of her death, and it was as if he had to make her pay for being his wife. He wanted her, he needed her, but he hated his need. He had a black soul."

Julie said slowly, "I don't think we'll tell our small Hugh of his great-grandfather. I don't think we'll tell Rafe. You haven't told him, have you, Edie?"

Edie paused in her work. She straightened in her chair and took off her glasses. She stared at Julie.

"Edie?"

After a moment Edie said slowly, "Not I. But I'm just wondering .... There was your father. He was never going to have you hurt, no more than you had been hurt. He hated Lucy's husband, Annie's father. He hated him worse than poison."

"He wouldn't have told Rafe?"

"It's a thing he might have done. In warning. In cold, straight warning. If it's in your blood ... you watch for it.

27

You keep it in irons. It's a thing he might have done, to tell Rafe in warning. He watched him like a hawk, that first three years before he let you and Rafe marry. Like a hawk. And never a sign of the bad blood did he see. He was as sure of Rafe as I am of you, my dear. But he was alone with Rafe, those long hours before he died up north. He was in great pain, and it may be that there, just before he died, he told Rafe. In warning. And the boy's been brooding on it."

Julie got up. She felt light, almost giddy. "I knew you had the answer," she said. "You've always had the answers."

CHAPTER THREE

THE DOORBELL RANG.

Edith Macrae said to herself, "Now who could that be?" and began to get out of her chair.

"It could be anybody," Julie reminded her with a smile. "The way everybody's been calling with flowers and kind words and anxiety …. I'll go, Edie." She moved on out to the hall and along to the door. She leaned and took a quick look through the narrow glass panel running down beside the door, put there by Hugh Macrae for the purpose of inspecting approaching visitors before the door was open. It was made of one-way glass, so that outsiders could not see in. The caller outside was a friend, a very old friend, Robin Sloan. Three years older than Julie, he was one of her first friends, one of the first people she had known. He had never married. Now he was not only friend; he had been the family lawyer since his father's death last year. He stood on the porch under the fanlight looking much more lawyer than friend tonight, his face steady and serious, a frown on his normally open brow.

Julie opened the door quickly. "Come in, Rob. How nice to see you!"

The frown disappeared like grime under a mother's washcloth, and he stepped across the sill. "I wasn't sure you'd be home."

"I'm home. Rafe's much better, and they're giving him something to keep him away under tonight."

"I'd have known he was better," Rob said dryly. He took off his gray gabardine coat and flung it down on the carved wooden chest against the inner wall. "Your eyes are shining again."

"Well," Julie said defensively, "it *has* been a long pull,

Robin. Maybe anybody's eyes would have stopped shining."

"Might be. You busy?"

"No. Edie is threatening to put me to bed, but I'm not really sleepy. I feel fine. Come on in. I think there's a cup of tea still in the pot."

He followed her into the room, greeted Edie, who liked him and showed her liking in her affectionate welcome, and sat down on the hassock Julie had vacated. He linked his hands together and looked from Edie to Julie through his tortoise-shell-rimmed glasses. Even at thirty-six he still looked undergraduate, with the big glasses, the loose tweeds, the careless tie. He said again, awkwardly, "I didn't know whether you'd be home or not, Julie."

"Well, I *am*, I told you I was. I'm here. You want some tea?"

"No. No thanks. So Rafe's better, is he?"

Edie gave him a sharp glance but said nothing. Julie sat down in the little slipper chair at the other side of the fireplace. "He may be conscious tomorrow," she said. "He may be quite himself again. It's—it looks as if that might come true."

"I see," Rob said thoughtfully. He ran a hand over his thick hair, mouse-colored and always awry. "That's nice," he murmured vaguely. "That's good." He got up abruptly and walked down the room to the window, touched the edge of the blue-and-silver brocade curtain, examined it carefully, came back again and sat down. "It looks a little as if it might rain," he remarked.

Over his bent head, Edie's eyes met Julie's in a question. Julie raised her eyebrows and shrugged a shoulder.

Edie said briskly, "Robin, you may as well come right out with it. What have you got on your mind? Are you lawyering or visiting or what? Is this call pleasure or business?"

Robin regarded her thoughtfully. "Both and neither. I didn't want to come. There's not much pleasure in it. As a friend, I'd have stayed away. As Sloan and Dawson, I had to come."

Julie said in a low voice, "You sound ominous, Rob. What is it?"

"Well—" he fixed his gaze on his knuckles. "This is the fourteenth of October. Tomorrow is the directors' and shareholders' meeting. At twelve o'clock. You were supposed to be there, Julie, to sign over to the new organization, the new company, your shares of the original Macrae stock."

She put a hand to her forehead. "I'd forgotten all about it. I'll be there, Rob. Of course I'll be there. It means so much to Rafe. He's worked so hard for this reorganization. But I'm glad you reminded me. I've been so taken up with him I'd forgotten."

Rob glanced at her quickly. His eyes, behind the spectacles, were miserable. He was a very kind person. What made him miserable?

"I ... well, Julie ... I don't think you ought to come."

Julie stared at him. His brown eyes met hers steadily.

Edie folded her work carefully and put it down on the table. She took off her steel-rimmed glasses and laid them on the red needlepoint. She folded her hands in her lap. The knuckles were enlarged. The veins showed on the backs, blue and heavy. She waited.

"Has something happened?" Julie asked, and her voice was quiet. Quieter than her heart, so apprehensive, always so fearful.

"No, not exactly. That is, not in the business. Everything's in order. All the proxies are in, all the organization is ready. Rafe had everything in shape."

"Is it that he ought to be there himself? Can't it go through without him?"

"No, there's nothing for him to do. It's you. Turning over your controlling interest in Macrae Enterprises to the new company ... to Rafe's new organization. You're the key figure tomorrow."

"Well, that's all right, Rob. We talked it all over long ago. It's a very sensible and profitable thing to do. Rafe has been working toward it for years. If my father were alive he would have done this himself. It's a sound, clear-headed, profitable move, to take in all the small companies he held, that Rafe's developed, to reorganize all the stock, to make one big company under one board of directors, one policy group, one head."

"Under Rafe."

"Of course, Rafe is the head now. He has been for six years, ever since father died. Of course, Rafe. Who else?"

Rob did not answer. After a moment, Edie said slowly, "There's more in this than meets the eye. Rob, there isn't any silly word around that Rafe has lost his mind through this car accident? You don't think he might have, since he's been unconscious so long? Do you have doubts that he'll regain his mental powers?"

Julie heard herself saying, "Have you been seeing Dr. Prescott? Is there something he hasn't told me?"

"No. Oh, Lord," Robin said prayerfully, and ran his fingers through his hair again. He lifted his head. "Look here, I'd rather burn in hell forever than do this, and if there were more time I wouldn't do it tonight. But tomorrow morning … And I don't think you should …. And we haven't had time to investigate …. And if it's not true you'll just have to forget it and forgive me, that's all … but I don't know what else to do."

"Very lucid indeed," Edie said dryly. "Your law training does you credit, my lad. Could you back up now and start over?"

Julie put her hand to her throat and made herself be still.

"Well," Robin said at last. "It's like this. You see … there was the matter of the car insurance. Something as small and simple as that. The insurance people came to us, naturally, to check. It looked open and shut. Of course Rafe carried all the insurance anybody can carry. And nobody else was involved. He didn't hit another car and he was driving alone. That's a bad stretch of road, there where his car went off. It looks as if he'd been driving pretty fast, but he certainly wasn't drinking. There was no smell of alcohol on him, and anyway everybody knows Rafe never takes a drink. So that's fine. It was eleven o'clock at night and he was driving fast to get home, and he swerved to let someone pass and his wheel caught the shoulder and the car went out of control and hit a tree, and he was flung through the roof and landed in a patch of fairly soft swamp, which is why he's here today. So that's open and shut."

"But?" Edie enquired.

"Julie, where had he been?"

"You know that, Robin. He'd been up at the cottage, putting the boats away, putting on the shutters, closing it up for the winter. He went up Saturday morning. He didn't really need to go, the caretaker could have gone over to the island any day. But you know how responsible Rafe was. And anyway, he said he had a lot of thinking to do about this reorganization and this would be a good chance."

"Why didn't you go with him?"

"Well, the baby, but mostly because of just that. He had some thinking to do. He carries a big load. He doesn't get much time to be alone."

"Did he go up to the island often, alone?"

"Not often. Sometimes. Four or five times a year, perhaps. I don't think I understand, Robin."

"I don't either," Rob said unhappily. "But ... the cottage is on an island, isolated, not overlooked by anyone else."

"That's why we've always loved it."

"And the whole district is deserted except between mid-June and mid-September. Did he go sometimes early in the spring, and late in the fall?"

"Oh, Rob, Rob! I've told you!"

"Well, to be blunt," Rob said at last, "he was alone when the car crashed. But he hadn't *been* alone. He wasn't alone when he got to Barrie. He had a passenger there. He had her at Bracebridge. They had coffee at a café. He took her on as far as Barrie, and there he took her to the bus stop and waited with her until the bus came. It was the bus to Toronto. He put her on it. Then he came on to Toronto alone."

The room looked very queer. It had a sort of ball of dark mist spinning in its middle.

"He didn't bring her on with him to Toronto, yet she was coming this way."

Edie said quietly, "The insurance people discovered all this?"

"Yes. They were bound to."

"Who was she? Have they any idea?"

"None. If there was more time, I'd make sure of her identity. I'd check everything. As it is, we're putting men on in the morning to try and trace her. That is—unless Julie countermands the order. After all, this is ... strictly from nothing to do with insurance."

"She must have been one of our neighbors," Julie said. "She must have been ... somebody from Echo Lodge, wanting a ride down ...." She stopped.

"In October?" He paused. "She was a tall girl, blonde, about thirty. She was dressed in a black dress, not countri-fied, and a short fur jacket. High heels. The man in the bus depot noticed the heels. And the legs. And the hair and the smile. And the husky voice."

CHAPTER FOUR

IT WAS HALF PAST NINE next morning when Julie got to the private patients' pavilion. She left her car on University Avenue, greeted the friendly doorman, and went up in the big elevator to Rafe's floor. There the air was weighted heavily with ether. Two operating-room wagons with sheeted patients had just emerged from the other elevator and moved down the corridor in front of her, propelled by probationers in their striped uniforms, sleeves rolled. Rafe's room was at the end, the corner room. Outside most of the other doors flowers drooped or stood pridefully in their ornate baskets or in vases, waiting to be taken into their owners' rooms after the night. Rafe's flowers were not outside his door. As she pushed it open she saw them, set neatly on his table and dresser, freshly tended, yellow chrysanthemums and bowls of asters, a vase of delicate African daisies, the usual masses of roses.

Miss Burnell was on duty, and just finishing the room, folding back the screen around the chaise longue. The green wool blanket across its foot was smoothly in place, its edges properly mitered. The windows were open a few inches, and the room smelled clean and orderly.

Julie went on through the inner corridor, between the washroom on one side and the clothes cupboard on the other, and emerged into the large bedroom. Rafe's bed was on her left. For a moment she was almost afraid to look toward him; that sick feeling of seeing a stranger in place of Rafe was heavy upon her. He was not a stranger, he was Rafe, her husband, but her mind had formed the idea somewhere, out of the strange voice, the strange words, the strange remoteness, and kept presenting it to her, as if it would save her from further fear and pain.

35

"Well, good morning, Mrs. Jonason," Miss Burnell said brightly. "I must say, you look better. You must have had a good night."

"I slept," Julie said. She *had* slept. She had taken the two pills Edie gave her without protest, and her mind had dropped into blank oblivion. She turned toward Rafe.

"Doesn't he look wonderful?" Miss Burnell asked. She came over to the bed. "I've given him his bath. Bandages off, prop his bed up six inches, doctor's orders. He had a wonderful night, Miss Baines said. Didn't mutter, didn't move. His pulse and temperature are normal. I'd say he was practically well—he might wake up sensible any minute."

Julie's hands clasped themselves round the brown metal bedrail.

It was Rafe, lying there peacefully. They had shaved the thick smooth fair hair on one side, toward the back, but he had his head turned a little on the pillow and the bare patch did not show very much. He was sleeping quietly, his face serene and relaxed, as she had seen him sleep at home. But not often. It was always Rafe who woke first, who waited for her to wake, whose active mind was immediately aware and bright when his eyes opened, as if his inner self relaxed only in the deepest and most necessary sleep, and then at once came on ... on guard duty?

She pushed the unhappy thinking away.

"Doesn't he look wonderful?"

"I can scarcely believe it, Miss Burnell. He's well. Isn't he? He's almost well."

"His body certainly is. You know, I keep thinking ... it's lucky he went out through the roof. So many people, when they're driving the car, get it through the chest. The steering wheel breaks off and they get it through the chest. But he hasn't got a mark on him, except that little bit of a crack in his skull. It really wasn't much. There isn't a thing wrong with him physically, now. It's just his mind that still has to get untangled, it's sort of scrambled, I guess, and after that wonderful rest last night I wouldn't be surprised if he came to his senses any second."

Julie thought, oh please, please, Rafe ... wake up and speak to me! I'm caught in a horrible, meaningless dream, and one word from you will clear it all away.

Robin's story about the girl was true. Robin would never have told it if it hadn't been true. But it didn't mean what he thought it meant. He had been right to be apprehensive. He had a very careful mind, and he would die in her interest any time. That she knew. His father and her father had been the closest friends, always having each other's complete confidence. Her father had once told her that he had hoped she might marry Robin Sloan. But of course ... she couldn't have married anyone but Rafe. Long ago, in those misery-filled years of her growing up, Robin had been a gentleman and he had tried to be kind; but with him as with all others she had been set apart, different. Until Rafe came. Now Robin had an extra protectiveness for her partly because he was trying to make amends. He was sensitive and kind and he was utterly honest. But he was drawing the wrong conclusions. There was no other woman in Rafe's life. It was utterly, utterly impossible. They were so close, Rafe and Julie, he and his wife; when they lay with their arms around each other, her head on his bare smooth shoulder, it was like being made whole, it was fearing nothing, knowing everything, it was like understanding God. That was as true for Rafe as for her; he had said so, in words, in gentleness, in ardor, in all the unconscious glances and touches and tendernesses—unconscious to him, but always known to her.

Miss Burnell was looking at her sharply. She said, "You'd better sit down, Mrs. Jonason. Maybe you slept, but you've had a long strain."

Julie smiled at her. She walked up along the bed, then, and put her hand over one of Rafe's, lying so relaxed on his breast. The tears stung suddenly behind her lashes. She

37

patted his hand quickly and went back to the wicker arm-chair in the corner of the room. She said steadily, "Has Dr. Prescott been in yet?"

"He'll be along any time, although he had a big operation this morning, a lobotomy. That takes a long time. It's a wonderful operation. I've been through a few with him." She went over to the dresser and settled her starched white cap on the gleaming hair. She took a small case of pancake make-up from her pocket and looked at Julie— "You don't mind?" and, at Julie's smile, smoothed out her complexion. She put the compact away, turned down her cuffs and buttoned them, slid her wrist watch on, then looked herself over in the mirror, her full-breasted figure, her slim waist and flat hips. Again engrossed, forgetful of her usual mask, she said almost absently, "It's too bad Dr. Prescott is so married."

Julie said carefully, "Is there a difference between married and *so* married?"

Miss Burnell looked at her, half-startled, and said with a laugh, "I shouldn't have said that. Only I *have* got a crush on that man, even at his age. He's so clever. All the nurses are crazy about him, so it's not really personal."

"Is there a difference?"

"Oh, *heavens!*" Miss Burnell sat down on the end of the chaise longue and looked at Julie. "I guess you never moved around in the world much, Mrs. Jonason. You married pretty young."

"Yes. I don't know very much."

"Well, I *do*. But it's just as well you don't. It's just as well all wives don't. You know, maybe that's what's the matter with things."

"What is?"

"Well, I mean to say … it used to be that girls married young, and they'd never been around, and so they didn't even suspect what could go on. So they were happy. And everything was neat and tidy, covered up and smooth. But when the world got so that the wives had been around too—if you know what I mean—well, believe me, when I get married I'm going to have eyes all over my head and halfway down my back. There isn't a man living that is going to fool me. I've been on the fanny-patted end for too long, if you'll excuse the coarseness." She put a hand down on the couch to prop herself, and looked at Julie straight, woman to woman. "You know, I hope you won't take any offense, but last night some of the girls and I were talking … it isn't anything you ought to mind, because nurses always talk over cases. And putting two and two together, me telling what a wonderful job Dr. Prescott had done on Mr. Jonason, and who he was married to, Juliet Macrae, Mr. Jonason, I mean, and how handsome he was, naturally someone else came up with something."

The cold fingers touched Julie's heart again. But she said gently, "Came up with something?"

"Yes … wasn't it you who had an operation, only five-six years ago … on your face? I mean to say … it isn't anything to mind now. It's all over. And there isn't even a scar. The other day I just caught a glimpse of a little pink line there along your cheek, down from the eye to the chin, but I cant see it now. The nurse who told us about it had been in the operating room. She said it was a new operation and everybody was scared stiff it wouldn't be successful, but it was, and your husband was wonderful about it. She said …"

Julie leaned her head back against the chair. After a moment she felt all right. "There was a … a thing on my face. It was there when I was born, quite small, but it grew as I grew. It was hideous."

"I'm sorry," Miss Burnell said evenly, and her hazel eyes met Julie's. They were not really hard. Maybe she was like lots of other people and had two layers, two surface coverings, not one. Maybe she wouldn't be a nurse at all, and such a very good one, if she were truly hard. It was a good thing to think. Julie felt oddly comforted. And she felt, too, that she must not draw back now. This was her chance to drag her old misery out into the fresh clean air, to face it.

She said, "It was a dark thing, rough and dark, almost black. It covered almost the whole side of my face."

"Well, you poor kid!"

"My father would have done anything to have it taken off, but when I was little, even when I was grown, there wasn't anything to be done. There was no safe operation."

Miss Burnell's eyes went to Rafe, to the perfect profile, the clear skin, the real sculptured beauty of his face lying on the pillow. "But he married you like that?"

The tears welled suddenly in Julie's eyes and brimmed over. They ran down her face. Miss Burnell got up abruptly. She got a Kleenex from the box on the dresser and came over to wipe Julie's eyes and face.

"Well, you poor kid," she said. "No wonder you're crazy about him. No wonder." She moved away, and then turned to look at Julie with appraising eyes. "You are certainly a pretty thing now, if you want to know. I was telling the girls last night—those big dark blue eyes, and that hair, so soft and curly, and as black as it comes—what I was kicking about," she said frankly, "was how crazy you are about your husband. No man's worth it, I said. And then Larson chimed in and told what he'd been like about that operation, just hanging over you, and so anxious ... and she said the thing was really awful, if you don't mind my saying so. Not a thing any woman could bear to live with. What I said, shooting off my big mouth, was, 'I guess he married her for her money!' But Larson said no. He acted clean gone over you. So maybe I am crazy, after all. Maybe I am. Maybe there is such a thing as love, although God knows men can sure put on an act."

Julie got up abruptly and went into the washroom. She bathed her face in cool water. She smoothed the little silky pad from her compact over her face and put on fresh lipstick. Coral, it was. She straightened her hair. She hadn't washed it after all, last night, but Edie has brushed it for fifteen minutes after she'd had her bath. She hadn't been very energetic last night, and Edie had treated her as if she were a child, helping her undress, getting her into the tub, putting on her flowered nightgown, taking her in by the hand to look at little Hugh, lying asleep in his crib. He slept on his front nowadays, with his head turned sideways and his thumb in his mouth. He was a beautiful boy, strong and fair and blue-eyed, with the eyes tipped a little at the outer corners just like Rafe's. Julie had almost an overwhelming need to pick him up and cuddle him, to hold him close in her arms, but she had turned away. He was so secure, this baby, so happy and secure. She could not communicate to him her dread, her fear, her blank unbelieving grief. Then Edie had given her the pills, propped her against her pillows and brushed her hair until she was too drowsy to sit up.

Her eyes met her own eyes in the mirror. She looked calm and steady now. It was hard to believe that such turmoil could go on in the human heart and soul and yet not show on the surface. She had not known it was possible. When people acted with serenity, apparently easy and relaxed, she had thought they were truly so. You could detect an act, she had always thought. You would always know when people were lying.

But would you?

The meeting was at twelve o'clock. Already it was past ten. If she did not go, Robin would be there; he would say she was with Rafe and that the whole thing of the merger would have to be postponed until Rafe was well.

If she did go, if she signed away her controlling interest in Macrae Enterprises, she would be affirming her trust and belief in Rafe. She *did* trust him. She *did* believe in him.

41

There were other people to be considered. Many other people rested in Macrae Enterprises. It had always been honest and good and clean. Her father had made it so.

Rafe was honest and good and clean. He had explained this merger to her a thousand times. There wasn't a flaw in it. It was co-operative, it was democratic, it was in the best interests of everyone. True, the control would no longer be in the hands of a Macrae, except as Julie was Rafe's wife and they were one, with little Hugh Macrae Jonason coming along to take over eventually. But it would be Rafe who had the ultimate control, whose signature, whose decisions would be final. That was only a matter of form.

He had been so good to her. Even when he had seen her first, he had been good. She had come downstairs with such reluctance to meet this boy from the West, this stranger who was to live with them and be tried out by her father, who had no son ... this lad who was a far-off cousin and so had a tiny bit of Macrae blood in him through his mother ... she had come downstairs with the familiar misery, waiting for the moment when his eyes would rest on her face and his whole being cringe and shudder away. But he had made no sign at all. He was only eighteen, an untutored boy from the British Columbia wilds, a tall, fine-looking boy, old for his age, strong, and with a freedom in his manner that she had never seen in anyone. And he had looked at her with those steady eyes, and smiled, and said, "So this is Julie! My mother would have liked to see you."

Julie had been fifteen, and she had fallen hopelessly, deeply, forever in love with Rafe at that moment. And, she knew later, her father had too, in his own way. There was nothing Rafe could have done which would more surely have endeared himself to her father. Nothing.

So—had ... Rafe been ... warned?

She swung quickly away from the mirror and went back to the bedroom. Miss Burnell had gone out, probably to get

Rafe's midmorning nourishment. He had been taking liquids through the glass straw for a long time now, and lately would swallow obediently what was put into his mouth with a spoon.

Julie went back to the armchair and sat thinking, her hand over her eyes. If only he would wake! If only he would say one word ... she would know him again. All the black pictures would go, the senseless fears, the hesitation, the insidious doubts. She was a creature of doubts and fears, which lay like an extra veneer on the basic caution of the Scot. One word from Rafe would send them flying. Now he was a man she did not know.

He moved on his pillow, and it seemed to Julie that he opened his eyes and then shut them again, not really waking. She got up softly and went to the other side of his bed, to stand there looking down at him. She put her hand out and laid it gently on his. Immediately he moved; he drew his hand away and flung it back to lie beside his head on the pillow. His eyelids moved again; the eyes almost opened. His lips moved, but he said nothing.

Miss Burnell came back into the room, and with her was Dr. Prescott, wearing his white operating-room coat and with a white surgeon's cap on his head. Tall and bony, with penetrating gray eyes and a firm mouth and chin, he did not look nearly as softhearted and as gentle as he really was. He was a famous specialist now, a brain specialist, but long ago when he was just beginning he had been the Macrae family physician. Except for her father and Edie, he was the first person Julie had ever seen. This man had attended her birth, thirty-three years ago, and had broken his heart trying unsuccessfully to keep her mother from dying after that birth. It was he who, at Rafe's insistence, five years ago, had cabled the British doctor about his new birthmark operation, who had persuaded him to come to Toronto and undertake it, who had assisted at the operation and that of four other patients, all grievously marked

43

at birth. Whenever he looked at Julie there was pride and satisfaction in his eyes, real happiness because of her happiness.

He put a hand now on her shoulder. He said, "I'd have expected him to be awake."

"He almost is," Julie said under her breath. She reached up and patted the warm hand.

"He hasn't been reacting exactly according to schedule. But the older I get the less I know about schedules. Human beings are so damned particularized."

Rafe moved again; a new kind of movement. It was as if he stiffened himself. He lay silent for a moment and then opened his eyes. He stared at the ceiling. Then, in a quick movement that bore in it no trace of weakness, he lifted himself, propped himself on an elbow. His eyes fell first on Miss Burnell, in her starched white; then on Dr. Prescott. His face tightened.

"Well," Dr. Prescott said. "So you're awake, my boy!"

Rafe looked at him without a trace of warmth. His mouth was tense. He said in a harsh, strange voice, "What is this place? Let me out of here!"

Dr. Prescott's hand fell from Julie's shoulder.

Julie put her hand out and caught Rafe's. He wasn't really awake yet. He was still lost. But he would know her.

She said, "Rafe, Rafe! Darling ... you were hurt. Rafe, you were terribly hurt! But you're well again now. Look at me! It's Julie, darling, it's Julie."

He looked at her. His eyes were like hard blue stones. He looked at her, at the nurse, the doctor, hemming him in. He looked back at Julie. He said, "And who the hell are you?"

CHAPTER FIVE

Four days later, on Friday, they brought Rafe home.

Julie had not seen him since that morning of his awakening. Dr. Prescott had not allowed it. Rafe was hostile; he had acted like a wild creature at bay, a thing from the safe darkness of the forest brought suddenly into civilization, terrified, belligerent, wary to the point of hatred. He did not know where he was; he did not seem to understand how he could be in a hospital, apparently perfectly well— if a little weak; he did not know Dr. Prescott, he knew no one. He would not talk, he sat in his bed listening, watching, never off guard for an instant.

"It's nothing to worry about," Dr. Prescott said, on that first morning and many times since. "He'll come out of it. He's not physically ill; there's no pressure on the brain. This is just the result of shock and the long unconsciousness."

But *he* was worried, Julie knew, for a day or two. Then Rafe's hostility seemed to die away, to be replaced by curiosity, by a certain acceptance of the situation, however puzzling it was. He became co-operative in many ways; he ate well, got out of bed, and moved about his room, and then walked the length of the corridor and back as often as he was allowed. He said practically nothing, but some of his wariness was gone and his anger seemed to have vanished.

It disappeared, the nurse reported, the first time he saw himself in the mirror. He had picked up a hairbrush in a natural way, as he stood there in his dressing gown, and turned to the mirror. He saw his face in the glass, and his shock must have been something like Medusa's when she saw herself reflected in the burnished shield; he turned to stone. Watching him covertly, the nurse reported that after a long time he put a hand up and touched his face experimentally; traced the lines beside his mouth, the fan of creases at the corners of his eyes, and last of all the streak of gray in his hair. He was only thirty-six, but that gray had been spreading over the left temple for ten years or more. He had put the brush down, then, and looked at his hands. Then he had gone to sit in the armchair, completely silent.

"He saw *age* in the mirror," the nurse had told Dr. Prescott shrewdly. "He knew then that we weren't all lying to him, that there were years between what he *really* was, what we'd been saying he was, and what he had been *thinking* he was."

He was easier to handle after that. But he wouldn't talk. He did what he was told, always watchful, accepted all suggestions, but he wouldn't talk.

It was on the evening of Friday that he came, because Dr. Prescott had wanted to bring him home, to observe his reactions. Julie sat with Edith in the living room, waiting, watching the clock. Robin Sloan was to come, too, as a casual visitor, someone who just happened to be there when Rafe arrived. What sometimes happened, the doctor said, was that the sight of a familiar face, unexpected, might suddenly snap the bands that held memory at bay, and bring a man's thinking straight again. It hadn't happened so far, but it would. Robin had suggested coming. He wanted to see Rafe. In everything connected with Rafe, he, Robin, was wary now too as he had never before seemed to be wary.

He came about seven, and was just inside the door when the doctor's car slid into the driveway. The headlights flashed across the inner wall, the dining room wall, and then were turned off. Julie got to her feet, her throat tight. Edie glanced at her but said nothing. Robin came in from the hall, having hung his coat away.

"I'll go to the door," Edie said. "I'm a familiar face

too. Surely the sight of us all together, here in this place ... surely the lad will know he's come home."

There were footsteps on the porch. Edie opened the door. There was a little silence. Then she said in an odd voice, "Rafe ... come in. It's good to see you."

Rafe did not answer. The doctor's voice said pleasantly, "Night, Edie. I've brought your boy."

"Yes, and welcome he is," Edie replied. But her voice wasn't right.

She came into the living room. Rafe followed her, Dr. Prescott behind them. Rafe stopped in the wide archway, looking quickly, sharply around him. His eyes arrived at Robin, and halted; but there was nothing in his expression except that early wariness. He summed Robin up by some secret measure of his own, and dropped him. He looked at the fire, at his own chair drawn up to it, and it meant nothing. He moved a little, and looked at Julie, standing in her blue dress—the dress he loved best, with its short cap sleeves and the square neck, the sapphire clips he had given her especially for the corners of that neckline. He said politely, in his own voice, but not with his own words or manner, "I guess we've met."

As he spoke, a certain relaxation came into the air. They had all been hoping, holding themselves in hope, but now the hope was gone.

Julie sat down slowly on the round blue hassock. Edie went across to her own chair. "Do sit down," she said, in the voice of an old automaton.

There was an armchair a foot or two in front of Rafe. He glanced at it hesitantly and then took it, lowering his tall body easily, with the familiar integration. Robin walked across the room and took a straight chair against the far wall. He sat stiffly there. Dr. Prescott went over to sit on the small sofa behind Julie. He said conversationally, "It's apparent you don't recognize this place, Rafe. It's your own home. The lady who let us in the door is Miss Edith

47

Macrae. This is her home too; it was once her brother's, who was Hugh Macrae, and who died six years ago. The gentleman beyond her is Robin Sloan, a very good friend of yours and also your lawyer."

Rafe's eyes, cool and cautious, had regarded Edie. They turned to Robin. At Dr. Prescott's last word he seemed to stiffen. He said, "So I have a lawyer, have I? What would you say I'd done, to need a lawyer?"

"You haven't done anything, my boy," the doctor's patient voice said. "You are the head of a very big business concern. Robin and his partners handle all your business affairs. His father before him did it for Hugh Macrae, and when Robin's father died Robin took over. He is your own age; he was your first friend when you as an eighteen-year-old boy came to Toronto eighteen years ago."

"So we're thirty-six," Rafe said coldly. "A very nice age, too." He set one knee across the other and swung his foot. "I can't say that I remember the gentleman and our beautiful friendship. It seems unfortunate."

There was a little silence. Then Rafe turned deliberately toward Julie. "I've seen this girl, of course. She was in my room the other morning. But you haven't given me the lowdown on who she is. Another of the Macraes, perhaps? And if so, how do I fit in here? I'm no Macrae."

Robin picked it up at once. He said quietly, "You know that, do you?"

Rafe flicked him a glance. "Certainly I know it. I know who I am. I'm no Macrae. I'm no Rafe Jonason, either, although you all keep saying so. I have to go along with you. What else can I do? There are some years missing. I admit that. I can't fill them in. But I know who I am. So now, who is the very pretty little girl in the blue dress with the eyes to match?"

Julie looked at him. After half a minute of looking she said in a low voice, "I am your wife, Rafe. I've been your wife for fifteen years, since you were twenty-one and I was eighteen."

He stared at her. There was not a trace of recognition in his glance, no warmth, no comfort, no allegiance, nothing. Nothing. At last he said, "This is a bit too much. You are *not* my wife! It's ridiculous."

Robin said evenly, "Why not?"

Rafe turned on him. "So a man can have a wife for fifteen years and forget her? Impossible. I've never seen this girl before. I don't know anything about her. I don't know her. For some crazy reason that I can't understand, you're all trying to trap me into something, into being somebody I'm not, into a setup I know nothing about."

Robin said dryly, "But a very nice setup. You must admit that."

Rafe said bitterly, "That's what I don't get. What is this, anyway? Who are you covering for? Why do you have to have a body? Who am I being a stooge for, taking a phony place? You're all trying to jam me into something, and I don't like it. How would you like it? I've been doped or something. None of this makes sense. I'm myself, I'm no stand-in for some queer guy who has mysteriously vanished."

Julie thought, This is not Rafe. He never used such words. This language is vulgar, hard, brutal. This is not Rafe. There *is* a mistake.

Edie, who had been sitting with her hands still, locked together in her lap, got up abruptly and went out to the dining room. There was a clink of glasses, some small meaningless sounds. The swing door to the butler's pantry opened and shut again, and then opened to let her return to the dining room.

Dr. Prescott spoke gently. "Rafe, let me explain, if I can. You had a bad accident, a severe blow on your head. You were thrown out through the roof of your car. You didn't land directly on your head, or your neck would have been broken, but you got a serious blow. It has affected your memory for a time. Somehow, in a way we do not yet fully understand, a part of your memory is shut off. We don't know enough about the brain. But I can assure you that you are indeed Rafe Jonason. I have known you ever since you came here and I have been your physician. In the past days I have examined you minutely, as you know, from head to toe. You have Rafe Jonason's body, although the mind may not yet be entirely his. It is all there, but locked away."

"What do you mean, Rafe Jonason's body?"

"Well, my boy, one of the first things I did for you was to take out your tonsils, that first winter you were here. They should have come out years earlier, but living as you did, in the wilderness with your father, the operation had not been done. I think I know my own work. You don't remember, but ten years ago you got an infection in your left forearm while you were away hunting and it was a serious infection which required deep lancing and produced an eventual scar. You have that scar. And last but not least, there is a scar of a large burn on your right thigh, a burn which you got when you caught a pan of boiling maple syrup out of the hands of a silly old woman up in the bush when you and Julie were there on a sugaring-off party. You caught the syrup because she was about to drop it where it would splash over a child, and in catching it you tipped the pan and poured a good cupful on your leg. It made quite a burn, which I subsequently dressed." He leaned back on the sofa.

Rafe's eyes searched the doctor's. His own face was pale. He said nothing.

Edie came back into the room. She carried a silver tray with glasses on it, glasses filled with liquid and tinkling with ice. There was a whiskey bottle on the tray, a flagrant thing, the label flaunting itself. Julie looked at her in amazement. Edie was strong temperance, and, even if she were not, even if she ever served liquor, she would never serve whiskey from a bottle when there were half a dozen of Hugh

Macrae's beautiful decanters available there on the shelf. Standing between her and Rafe, looking down at her, Edie said firmly, "I know we all need a drink. That's yours, dear, I made it as you like it."

Julie took the glass numbly. Edie turned to the doctor, who took his without question. Hugh Macrae had always given liquor to his friends. She went to Robin, who was obviously startled, but who took his glass, and since Edie planted herself firmly between him and Rafe, his shock was not seen. She went finally to Rafe and held the tray before him. "Your favorite brand," she said, to a Rafe who had never to anyone's knowledge touched liquor, not even when Hugh Macrae was alive and had offered the boy a drink every night of his life. "I made it pretty weak," Edie said. "Maybe you'd like to fix it."

Rafe did not see that all eyes were upon him. He took the tray as a natural thing. He took the glass. He took the bottle. He held the glass up to the light, measuring the strength of the liquor, and expertly poured out another two fingers into his glass. He said grimly, "Well, at least this makes sense, anyway," and drank half his drink at one swallow.

Edie went back to her chair. She set the tray down on her table and lifted her glass carefully.

Julie drank her ginger ale. She was lost, hopeless. Rafe finished his drink. He sat silent, staring at her. A little color came into his face. Dr. Prescott sat thoughtfully, tapping a fingernail on the edge of his glass. After a moment he got up.

"I think I'd better see you in bed, my boy," he said gently.

Edie got up too. "I'll come," she said briskly. "I've laid out his things in the yellow room, Nat. I'll come and turn on the lights."

Rafe got up without protest. His long legs unfolded, he stood tall and slim in his gray suit. His face was flushed.

The doctor took his arm and they walked out into the hall, toward the staircase. The three of them went up together.

Julie set her glass down carefully. She dropped her face into her hands. She heard Robin get up and cross the room to her. She felt his kind arm around her shoulders. He patted her gently, over and over. He sat down on the sofa beside her.

She lifted her head. She said, "It isn't Rafe. This man is not Rafe."

"That's what Edie was proving. Smart girl."

"He isn't Rafe, Robin."

Robin got up and walked up and down the floor. "I'm very strongly tempted to agree with you. Except that …"

"Except that what?"

"Well, if it isn't," Robin turned and came to stand in front of her, his face heavy with thought. "If he isn't, Julie, this is the biggest and smartest double bluff—or triple bluff—I ever heard of. It's just impossible. He's got to be Rafe."

"But he isn't. Rafe couldn't talk the way this man talks. Rafe never used such words, even when he first came, when you might have expected them, when he'd been mixing with rough men all his life. He was always quiet, very restrained in his speech, gentle, kind. This man is cold and cruel and hard, Robin. He isn't Rafe. And if he isn't …" Julie said from the depths of despair, "if he isn't, *where is Rafe?*"

Robin sat down in the chair Rafe had vacated, and looked at Julie, his hands under his chin. "You couldn't fake the evidence Dr. Prescott gave."

"Yes, you could. If you were determined. You could fake a scarred arm and a burned leg, if you knew about them. Everybody's had his tonsils out, and Dr. Prescott could be mistaken."

"He'd have had to start a long time ago, Julie."

"Then, he did. It's someone who has been meaning to step into Rafe's place for a long time. It's someone who has been watching Rafe, doing the things Rafe did, getting ready. I'm sure, Robin. This man can't be Rafe. Rafe would … he would *know* me, Robin."

Robin shook his head. "He couldn't have faked the hospital stuff. He was really out. He really had a fractured skull and concussion. There wasn't any fake there."

After a moment Julie said, "No. No."

"And if he's an imposter, trying to get into Rafe's shoes, why doesn't he just do it, then? We're all handing him the shoes on a silver platter."

Julie pressed away the lump in her throat. Her mind turned this thing over, turned it and twisted it as you turn a piece of glittering stone under a light.

"Robin."

"Yes, dear?"

"Robin, it wasn't Rafe who left the cottage. It was this man. The—the woman. She wasn't with Rafe. She was with this man." She was groping, but something was beginning to make sense. "There wasn't supposed to be an accident. It was Rafe who went up to the cottage, all right. I know that." She remembered the tenderness of their parting. She stopped for a minute and steadied herself again. "It was Rafe who went to the cottage, but it wasn't Rafe who left it. That woman … she was never in Rafe's life. And there wasn't supposed to be an accident. But there was; and then this man, this awful stranger, he *has* lost his memory. Don't you see? He doesn't know why he's here. It was all planned, but he doesn't know. He knows who he is, he knows perfectly well. And he knows there's something terribly wrong about the whole thing. He's got a glimmering of a plot. He knows who he is, someone who is wicked and cruel and dishonest, who has always known plots. He knows there would be a plot. But he's lost the threads. He doesn't know what to do! Don't you see? Oh, Robin, don't you see?"

He stared at her. He took off his glasses and polished them. He put them on again.

"It makes sense, Robin. It does."

He said slowly, "And the substitution was to take place just before the big merger, so this man would be in control from the start. It would be easier then, too; there'd be new business procedures, new men. Easier for him to grope along and fool people. Maybe even the accident was partly faked; there was supposed to be an accident, but nothing so serious."

"What makes me so sure," Julie said, "is that girl. The tall blonde girl. She wouldn't have been in Rafe's life."

"Oh," Robin said abruptly. "She wasn't. I mean … she's been identified. That's squared away. She wasn't anybody. I mean, she was the bus driver's wife. She used to be a waitress at Echo Lodge. Her name is Mabel Burns. You know her."

Julie said slowly, "Yes, I know Mabel Burns. But she … Rafe …"

"There isn't any she and Rafe. She was in the café in Bracebridge, having coffee. Rafe came in. She hailed him. He knew her. She asked him if by chance he was driving south, that her husband's bus was coming up as far as Barrie and then he was taking the southbound bus back. Her husband, I mean. She had been up visiting her mother and was on her way to Barrie to ride home with her husband. It's as simple as that. She was nobody."

The dark pain lifted from Julie's heart and then settled again. Suddenly nothing made any sense. Nothing made any sense at all.

Edie and Dr. Prescott came downstairs. They came into the living room. Edie's lips were pressed together and her color was high. "He's in bed," she said shortly. "He's wearing Rafe's pyjamas. Rafe's slippers fit him. He took his wrist watch off and laid it on the night table, just the way Rafe always did."

"Edie," the doctor said patiently, "this man *is* Rafe. How can I convince you?"

"You can't. Not unless you turn Presbyterian and admit that by the doctrine of original sin our Rafe has had a devil locked in his heart all these years and it's just got loose and got control of him! So there, Nat Prescott! Will you admit that, man?"

"In a way, I will. Yes, I will. I'll admit it scientifically. I'll say that you can have a dual personality. That for long years, all your life, you can put away from you all the wrongdoing, all the harshness, all the evil, all the weakness, and shut it in a tight casket in your mind. You can deny it, refuse to allow it. What shows, the rest of you, is your best self: good and clean and honest and loving and true. I can admit so much. I can go further and say that there are kinds of upbringing that force a human being to shut away too much of himself—innocent sins, small pleasures made wicked by someone, false standards, a morality impossible to human realization—so that too much of the whole being has to be locked away in order to win approval. You follow me?"

"I certainly do, sir," Robin said.

"Well, then—at a point—there's a break-through. The shut-off personality is so big that it is bigger than the real one. There is too much power locked away; too much has been denied. It could have been made part of a whole, that darker side; its tiny facets could have been met with day by day as if it were not evil but human, to be accepted and dealt with bit by bit, changed. Transmuted. But if it wasn't ... then some day there can be a break-through. In this accident it happens that a barrier has been built between the two sides of Rafe's personality. You understand? And the hidden side has come up. That's all."

Edie said obstinately, "This man is not Rafe."

"This man is Rafe," Dr. Prescott said. "My God, Edie, do you think I'd bring him here if I weren't sure? This man is Rafe Jonason! And he is not mad. He is not remotely insane. He is confused, but he is not mad, nor dangerous. He is angry and puzzled, but he is not mad. He has to be brought back to himself, we all want that, and it's home and love that will do it." He looked at Robin. "There is a couch outside that bedroom door," he said. "Will you sleep there tonight, Rob? If he isn't himself in the morning we'll look the situation over. He won't stir, but I think these two doubting Thomases might be happier if you were here."

CHAPTER SIX

THE NIGHT OF RAFE's homecoming was one of the longest
Julie had ever known. She lay in the wide bed in the room
that had been hers and her husband's and stared at nothing in the darkness, not moving. The nights of her youth
had been long, when life stretched away lonely and bleak
and empty, when she had been realizing deeply, hour after
hour, how little there was for her in the world. Physical
comfort, yes; she had that. Love, too, from her father and
from Edie. But no gaiety, no fun, no easy moving about
with people, no theater, no concerts, no travel, no friends.
She could do needlework, and had learned to sew beautifully. She could manage a house, and cook, and arrange
flowers. She had read a great deal, and she was a good
pianist. Her music meant a great deal to her. Actually, as
she had always told herself, she had a very great deal, more
than most people had in most ways. But she had been a
prisoner, a prisoner of her own thoughts and fears—and,
of course, with extra bars forged by the feelings of others.
For a stranger to see her unexpectedly was to have a day
ruined; to see her face, she understood, was to acquire a
horrible, unforgettable memory, to sense fear. The nights
when she had been growing up had been bad, there was
no doubt about that; but surely this was worse. When she
analyzed it she knew that her emotion in those days and
nights had been fear and sorrow for herself, colored only
slightly with concern for her effect on others. Now it was
absolute terror for Rafe—and perhaps through him, her
son. Rafe's son; little Hugh.

What was he, this man with Rafe's body? Who was
he? It was as if the devil himself had entered into that body

and possessed it. Could that happen? When the mind lost its control, was there a devil who sprang in and took over, gloating at his power, smashing down every good and kind impulse, every clean word and thought, every smile, every hope, everything sweet and warm and loving? Old books were full of demoniacal possession; was it true, could it happen, had it happened to Rafe? Because … it might be Rafe's body that slept in the yellow room—in the room that long ago had been his mother's, Annie's—it might be Rafe's body that lay in the comfortable bed, relaxed under the doctor's strong medicine, but it was not inhabited, that body, by Rafe's soul.

The creature downstairs in the early evening, who looked and moved and spoke as if it were Rafe, that creature *had* no soul.

What is soul?

At one point during the night she got up and went to the shelves of books in the alcove into which was set the wide front window of her room. There was a soft, low chair in the alcove, and a good light. Before her marriage she had spent many sleepless nights there, reading and reading. She found her Thorndike.

"Soul … the part of the human being that thinks, feels, and makes the body act; the spiritual part of a person … energy of mind or feelings; spirit: *his writing has no soul* … the essential part."

She sat in the low chair for a long time, her bare feet curled under her, the quilted silk cover which lay folded over the back of the chair pulled around her. Energy … thinking, feeling, doing. The body could not function at all without a soul, so there was something in that strong familiar body of Rafe's, something that gave it life. But it was not the soul she knew.

Her bedroom door opened softly, and she sat up in the chair, her heart leaping in her breast.

It was Edie, her white hair flying, her red dressing gown

clutched around her, her chubby little feet silent in their red velvet slippers. She closed the door noiselessly behind her and came down the long room, over the thick, soft, white carpet. She came into the alcove. "This is where I thought you'd be," she said. She came quickly and put her arms around Julie. "I'm frightened too," she said. "We'll just have to be frightened together. It's no use not facing up to it. It's never any use."

At eight o'clock Miss Burnell arrived in a taxi, sent by Dr. Prescott. Robin had got up from his couch in the wide hall outside Rafe's door, and he bathed and shaved in the small bathroom off the empty room next to Rafe's and came down to breakfast tidy and clean, if a little haggard and grim around the eyes. They sat in the small breakfast room, he and Edie and Julie, and ate bacon and toast and drank coffee in silence. At a distance, from the kitchen, small Hugh's bright voice could be heard. But Julie had told his nurse not to bring him in to breakfast with her. Small children sense trouble too easily.

She said, "Did Rafe stir at all?"

"Didn't hear him. I turned my couch around and had it smack in front of his door, in case he got up. But he didn't. He was up early in the bathroom off his own room, so I turned the couch around again when I heard the water running. He wouldn't like it," Robin said evenly, "if he knew we didn't trust him."

"You didn't sleep much, I gather."

He grinned at her and at Edie. "I don't suppose any of us did." He drank his coffee and set the cup down. "I've got an idea, for what it's worth," he said. He got his leather cigarette case from his pocket, glanced at Edie and Julie, took out a cigarette and lit it. "I think it's worth a good deal. I think there's someone who can help us, all the way down the line. I'd like to go and see him this morning, and I wish you'd come, Julie."

"How can anybody help us? It's Rafe who needs help. What can we do?"

"You convinced this man is Rafe?"

Julie looked at her hands. "How can I be convinced of anything? I keep remembering how sure Dr. Prescott is. I keep trying to make sense in my own mind. I don't know what I think."

Edie said firmly, "It isn't Rafe." She pressed the button under the table and got up. "Jennie wants to clear away," she said, and led the way into the study, across the hall. It had been Hugh Macrae's retreat. A long, wide room, lined with books, with two wide, soft, red-leather sofas and half a dozen easy chairs, bright with daylight from a window which took up the whole back wall, it had been built on to the end of the stone house twenty-five years ago but was still called "the new room." Rafe used it for a home office. The polished desk with its end against the farther wall stood shining and empty.

Julie sat down in the corner of one of the sofas and pulled down her gray skirt. Edie took the smallest of the easy chairs and sat stiffly erect. Robin stood in the middle of the floor, looking up at the fine painting of Hugh Macrae hanging in the open space between the book shelves.

Edie said, "Who is this man who can help us?"

"Well," Robin answered thoughtfully, "he's rather a remarkable person. You'll have heard of him, perhaps. I know him slightly. I've heard him give evidence in court a good few times. He's a psychologist by trade, lectures a bit at the University. His name is Merrill ... Dr. Jonathan Merrill." He gave Julie a quick glance.

After a moment she said, "He has something to do with the police."

"Well, yes. Yes, in a way, he has."

Edie bent and plucked a thread from the dark red carpet. She sat up again with a flushed face. "It's never a foot in this house the police have come," she said. "We've been law-abiding folk since the beginning. We're no cattle-stealing Lowlanders."

Julie looked at her abruptly. Her mind began to turn over and over. Cattle-stealing Lowlanders. Rafe's grandfather ...

Robin knew the family history, but the detail of this reference had not been made clear to him. He answered Edie. "I'm not suggesting it's a police matter, Edie. Maybe it isn't. On the other hand, maybe it is. If Rafe is Rafe ... if this man is Rafe... it's obviously a medical problem, or however they'd classify it. Physical. Maybe even surgical, although Prescott says there's no pressure. But if this man *isn't* Rafe ... then it's definitely something for the police."

"He isn't an imposter ... he isn't trying to pretend he's Rafe, Robin. He isn't doing anything under false pretences."

"You sure about that?" He walked over and dropped his ash in the tray on the desk. "This thing's got more possibilities than a game of chess. If a man wanted to get himself in here in Rafe's place, I can't think of a smarter piece of business. I figured that out in the silent watches of the night, so to speak. It's a new slant. Suppose there was a substitution ... planned out cleverly for years. This imposter is going to have a terrible time to *be* Rafe, in this very intimate home situation. He might be able to manage the business stuff. I wouldn't be surprised if he'd make rather a good showing there. There may even be someone inside the organization who's been selling information, who stands ready to help ..."

"No, Robin."

"We'll have to be tough," Robin said grimly. "We have to take everything into consideration. There are about three million dollars in the kitty; I added that up in my dreams, too. And lots more could be made, with a sharp, unscrupulous operator at the head of Macrae's. God only knows what the plot is. I can see ten miles ahead and see how they

61

could use Macrae's—if there is a 'they'— Macrae's, with its fingers in every country in the world, with its reputation for integrity. It would be worth grooming a man for years to get him into Rafe's shoes. But he'd have a bad time taking over here in the house. This might be the smartest way to do it. If I'm right," he said angrily, "this phony gentleman will begin to capitulate in a few days … he'll begin to remember … he'll begin to *be* Rafe again. And we'll all be so relieved—and the change will be so marked, comparing him to what he was last night—that we'll forget the standard. We'll forget Rafe. We'll be fooled."

"I couldn't be fooled, Robin."

"Julie, Julie, you could. Because you want to be. And because you love Rafe, and you know he's been hurt, and you're so gentle and forgiving … and he's little Hugh's father … and even when … well, even when he's making love to you," Robin said, and was angry, "you'll make allowances. And gradually you'll forget the real Rafe. There's the danger, Julie. There's the danger."

They looked at each other. In that minute Julie knew what she had never known before; that Robin loved her.

Edie said, "The boy's right. Who is this man, you say, Robin? Does he wear a uniform, if he's to do with the police? Do we have to put up with the shame of the blue uniform, here in this house?"

Robin turned to her with relief. "It won't be that, Edie. I'm sure. He's a wise man, sensitive and kind and wise. I've heard him give evidence, I know. It seems to me he's right for us; he's a psychologist by training; he understands the mind as perhaps even Dr. Prescott doesn't, who is, after all, a surgeon. The *human* workings of the mind, the emotional, not the physical structure. And maybe he can give us some insight into Rafe's actions. Then, if we are dealing with an imposter …"

Julie got up. "I'll go," she said.

CHAPTER SEVEN

DR. JONATHAN MERRILL lived and worked on Prince Albert Street, one of the old streets in the North Annex, lined with houses of old Toronto. Robin had telephoned, and Dr. Merrill was at home and would be pleased to see them. They got out of Robin's Buick and went up the walk through Jonathan Merrill's garden, to twist the old-fashioned bellpull on the front door of the long wing at the east.

It was a policeman who came to the door, and Julie's courage faded a little. He was a young man, tall and exceedingly erect, with a nice, firm thin face under dark hair and a pair of dark eyes that held intelligence and a look of integrity. He had on a blue uniform, shoulder strap and belt.

"Mrs. Jonason?" he asked pleasantly. "Mr. Sloan? Dr. Merrill is expecting you. May I take your coats?"

They went through a small hall into a huge room, the whole of whose center was taken up with a desk made of three immense tables pushed together. The papers, books, documents on the tables looked orderly, and were probably segregated into various interests, but the amount of work suggested was tremendous.

Dr. Merrill was standing at a window at the far side of the room, a long window which reached all the way to the floor. He was holding a photographer's negative up to the light. He turned. He was thin and rather tall, although not as tall as Rafe; he had a pale face with hollow cheeks, surmounted with a thick thatch of graying auburn hair, curly and obviously unmanageable. But his distinguishing feature was his eyes. Large and brilliant, they were beautiful eyes, the sort of eyes that saw everything, but with kindness and a clarity that would see through to a truth that would surely be a good truth, as the deep truth is always good.

The eyes rested on Julie and then on Robin, and before he spoke he gave a little nod, as if he had been communing with himself.

His voice was beautiful, too, very quiet, but sonorous and gentle. Julie told herself, "I am not afraid. I am not afraid."

The police constable mentioned their names. Dr. Merrill came forward, but he did not offer to shake hands. He repeated the names, then moved his hand vaguely toward a grouping of sofa and chairs around a small corner fireplace in which coal burned with a red glow. The policeman left them unobtrusively and went to sit at the far side of the big table, to bend his head over a big piece of paper, a chart or something of the sort, upon which he was making check marks as he consulted a notebook.

Julie and Robin sat in opposite corners of the shabby old sofa. Jonathan Merrill took the armchair, got out his cigarettes with hesitant, almost vague movements, held the box out to Julie, who shook her head; to Robin, who accepted and produced a lighter. He bent forward. He said, "I'm sure you know who we are, Dr. Merrill. They say you have quite a penchant for collecting people and information about them."

"One of those tropical plants," Jonathan Merrill murmured. "Flytraps? Is that it?"

Robin grinned. He had a boyish grin that took away the rather scholarly remoteness of his face. "All right, flytrap," he agreed. "What you can't know is that Mrs. Jonason's husband, Rafe Jonason, is ... well, you may remember the accident he had a couple of weeks ago, almost three weeks ago?"

Jonathan Merrill nodded.

"He had a small skull fracture and concussion. He's been in hospital until last night. The doctor brought him home last night, Dr. Nathaniel Prescott. You'll know him well."

"Yes."

Robin said carefully, "I don't quite know where to start. Rafe hasn't … he isn't … well, there's something still wrong with his mind. He isn't himself. He—well, he doesn't know any of us. He doesn't know his wife. He finds his home completely unfamiliar. He doesn't know why he's there, or seem to have any memory of it at all." He stopped. "What's worse is that none of his reactions are right. He is an entirely different man from the Rafe Jonason we have known."

Jonathan Merrill looked at Julie.

"Actually," Robin went on, "there is *too much* difference."

"In what way?"

Robin fumbled in the pocket of his plaid tweed coat and found the clean handkerchief Edie had given him that morning. It was one of Rafe's, but he didn't know it. He blew his nose. "Well … the Rafe we knew never drank. He never took a drink under any circumstances that we know of. He was exceptionally clean-living, controlled, sane, directed. Last night Miss Macrae, Julie's aunt, who doubts him strongly, produced drinks. Rafe not only accepted, he accepted as if he were more than familiar with liquor, glad of it, in need of it, accustomed to relying on it in moments of crisis. The man we know did not have these attitudes toward liquor. He kept it in the house, served it, lived with it always in his business life, but he just didn't drink. There was no sense in drinking, he said flatly, and he didn't drink. I may as well admit that his attitude gave me a good deal of perspective on the subject, so much so that I rarely drink myself."

Jonathan Merrill leaned forward with his hands loosely clasped between his knees. "What made Miss Macrae offer him liquor?"

Julie looked at Robin. "I think it was Rafe's voice," she said. "The inflections are wrong. She could have un-

65

derstood forgetfulness … weakness after being ill. But his voice isn't right. He … he … the echoes are wrong."

Jonathan Merrill regarded the smoke curling up from his cigarette.

"What does Dr. Prescott say?"

"He says that this man is Rafe Jonason. He has examined him physically." Robin went into detail. Merrill listened.

"You are certain that he is satisfied? He has no secret doubts?"

"Quite certain."

"Dr. Prescott is an authority. There is no one better."

"But there are people who look almost identically alike. The scar on the infected arm, the burned leg, the tonsil operation … they could be faked. None of them can be proved by X ray."

After a moment Dr. Merrill said, "You suspect a long-term plan of substitution?"

There was silence.

"Henry."

The policeman got up at once and came forward. Jonathan Merrill said, "This is Police Constable Lake. You may be assured of his discretion. It would appear that he should be making notes. If we are dealing with anything in the area of substitution, action will be necessary. You have no objection?"

They all looked at Julie.

She shook her head.

P.C. Lake got a notebook from his side of the table and came back, to sit at the other table, facing Dr. Merrill.

"As I remember," Dr. Merrill said slowly, "Mrs. Jonason is the daughter of Hugh Macrae, who started Macrae Enterprises some forty years ago in a very small way, having just come out from Scotland. His daughter Julie was his only child, her mother having died at her birth. Macrae never remarried. The child …" He looked at Julie

66

sharply, as if something he had not expected had come into his memory.

Julie said steadily, "I had a disfiguring birthmark on my face. My father was brokenhearted. He spent a great deal of money trying to find some way to have it removed, but there was nothing to be done. Five years ago my husband heard of a new operation and it was done with success." She stopped. "My father had been dead then for only a year."

Jonathan Merrill gave that small confirming nod of his. He got up and poked a little at the fire. He sat down again. He went on. "Hugh Macrae, therefore, had no son. There was no one to inherit the small empire he had built. His daughter ..."

"Was not likely to marry," Julie finished. "That is true."

Dr. Merrill said under his breath, "It is always easier to work with a realistic approach. Very well, his daughter was not likely to marry. And Macrae was a Highlander, with a strong sense of family, of the linking of generations. So he looked about him, and at a point hit upon the idea of the son of a remote cousin, this Rafe Jonason, who had Macrae blood through his mother, and who was an orphan with no prospects. The boy's mother had died years before, the father was killed in a lumbering operation when the boy was in his late teens. Macrae sent for him."

"You have a good memory," Robin said.

"It was a dramatic story, and much discussed in the city. The element of romance always captures the human imagination. I know very little more, except that young Jonason exceeded his kinsman's highest expectations in the business world, being a young man of great native judgment and shrewdness, and also that Macrae became personally fond of him. It would seem that the daughter, too, found him to be a fine person, and with her father's wholehearted consent, married him." He looked at Julie suddenly, almost startled, as if a thought had stabbed him. She could not read his mind.

He said, "Tell me how this accident occurred."

Robin told him in complete detail. He left out nothing, not the blonde girl who had turned out to be the bus driver's wife, nothing.

Merrill said, "The highway police picked him up? How soon after the accident?"

"Not more than a few minutes, sir. He was only a few miles south of Barrie, and a truck driver saw the accident and phoned in immediately from a gas station. Also he himself, the truck driver, went back to the accident and stayed with Rafe, not touching him. If there was any substitution," Robin said evenly, "it was not at that point."

"What has been done up at the cottage? Has it been examined?"

"No."

Merrill looked at P.C. Lake, who went on writing.

"What about fingerprints?"

Robin got up suddenly. "I guess I'm a fool," he said. "I never thought of fingerprints."

Merrill looked at P.C. Lake again, and said, "Dentistry."

Robin sat down. "I'm a fool," he said again.

"Such proof will solve only one problem, that of the physical identity. There will still remain the dissociation, the split in the personality."

"Can it be cured?"

"It responds to treatment. There are well-authenticated cases of such dissociation."

"May I give you Dr. Prescott's analysis, sir?"

"It will be valuable."

Robin repeated Dr. Prescott's words … his explanation of the shut-off aspects of personality, suppressed, inhibited, and their eventual break-through. Merrill listened. "He is quite right," he said. "There are more involved factors, but that is a very clear and straightforward exposition." He glanced at Julie. "It troubles you?"

"Even if he were cured," she said with difficulty, "there would always be the ... the memory of this other man.... He seems hard, cruel, bitter, vindictive, coarse.... Where did he come from? I don't understand. Are we all two souls, warring in one body? Are we all in danger of this awful cleavage? Do we all have two lives? I can't ... All last night I kept seeing this new face. It has evil in it. Evil!"

Robin reached over absently and took her hand. He unclenched the fingers. He said to Merrill gently, "She has led a sheltered life, as you may imagine. And her perception was shaped by pain and fear and loneliness. For which," he said coldly, "I blame myself."

"Why?"

"I could have been her friend. When Rafe came ... he showed no shock at ... at the thing which the rest of us ... the thing which hurt her so much, cut her off from life. He showed no shock. Why was I so small, so childish, so blind, so ..."

Jonathan Merrill leaned back in his chair. "Just a moment. You say Rafe showed no shock at first sight of this very lovely girl with her very grave disfigurement? No shock. How old was he?"

"Eighteen."

"I find that odd." He looked at Julie. "You would have been expecting shock. You would be familiar with the natural responses of others. You would have been watching his eyes. You are sure? There was no withdrawal, instantly concealed?"

"None."

He said, "Then he was forewarned. He was prepared. How?"

Julie said, "I thought that out last night, too." She opened her purse and brought out a bundle of letters, old letters, tied with a faded piece of blue tape. "These are let-

69

ters that my aunt Edith wrote to Rafe's mother. They were very fond of each other, and although Annie ran away to marry Lief, Rafe's father, there was no real estrangement. It was unnecessary and Annie soon wrote home. She was happy with Lief, but lonely so far away, and she and Edie wrote constantly. Edie would have gone to visit her if it had not been for me, but I could not go and Edie would not leave me. My father went once, when Rafe was about seven. He was impressed with the little boy then. I was four. There was close contact between Annie and my aunt Edie and my father. Annie knew all about my birthmark, it's all in the letters."

"Rafe's had access to these letters?"

"Yes, he brought them with him when he came. He had read them thoroughly, trying to visualize his new home and all of us. I have always known that, but it didn't register that he would have prepared himself for the shock of seeing me. I thought … I felt … It was so heavenly to be looked at as if …"

Jonathan Merrill said thoughtfully, "You are beautiful now. You have character as well as beauty."

"Thank you," she said, and then answered his deeper thought. "I am not sorry for myself now in any way. But I am still apprehensive and too watchful, too aware. I have to be careful about that."

"You had a great feeling of security in your husband."

"Absolute security."

"And this man is a stranger."

"If he is Rafe, and if he gets better," Julie cried, "where does *this* personality go? Where does this cold, wild, vicious personality go? Does it hide itself again, so that at any moment it may emerge? Does it live, does it stay on in existence?" She leaned back. "I couldn't bear it."

Robin said, "Sir, what is the cure?"

Jonathan Merrill got up and walked to the window.

He looked out over the leaf-strewn lawn behind his house. He said mildly, "It can be rather involved. My own feeling is that it is a matter of fusion … a matter of realizing that we have to deal with two parts of a whole man, which do not accept one another; and we have first to make one part, whichever is in control at the moment, see that the other exists and accept the fact of its existence; and then gradually, bit by bit, get one part to face the other and either accept or reject each very small aspect of the other."

"Maybe I don't understand very well," Robin decided.

"Take it this way. The Rafe you know seems to have lived a life very close to perfection. He did not drink. Had he other vices?"

"None," Julie said. "None. He hadn't even a temper. He was perfect. He was a wonderful person, sweet and good and kind and thoughtful and clean and loving and perfect. He was simply perfect."

Jonathan Merrill said, "Nobody can be perfect." Then, "I take it that your house is carefully run? Everything orderly, smooth, good? And I gather that as head of your father's business your husband's responsibilities would be great? And it seems obvious that as a husband he has made you happy. Do you understand what I am saying?"

Julie looked at Robin. He understood. He said after a time, "The other side of the mirror, Dr. Merrill?"

"Something like that. Perhaps." He considered. "If this is the physical body of the true Rafe Jonason …" He stopped. His eyes looked startled again. He went on. "If this is the physical body of Rafe Jonason, there are still a number of possibilities. We may have a true dissociation— the other side of the mirror, as you suggest, Mr. Sloan. Or we may have … conscious rebellion. That I doubt; there is too much at stake. Or …."

Robin interrupted. "Something we have omitted to tell you," he said. "Just how much was at stake."

Dr. Merrill looked at him inquiringly.

Robin went into the subject of the business merger. He made it all very clear. From time to time Jonathan Merrill nodded, or glanced at Police Constable Lake, or fitted the tips of his fingers together. Robin finished.

An inner door opened and a maid in a black uniform with neat white collar and cuffs came in with a coffee tray. She set it down on the table between Julie and Dr. Merrill and departed silently, without so much as a glance at the visitors. Merrill glanced at Julie, who bent forward and poured the coffee automatically into the four pottery cups. Merrill got up, put four lumps of sugar and much cream into one cup and carried it to P.C. Lake. He took another cup for himself, black and clear. Julie put cream into Robin's cup.

Dr. Merrill said abruptly, "You say that Rafe's mother did not have to run away with his father, that Macrae would have allowed them to marry and given them his blessing?"

"That's really true. It was just that Annie, Rafe's mother, had had a miserable childhood because her own father, back in Scotland, was dreadful to her mother, cruel and selfish, and she never quite got over the memory, my aunt Edie thinks. My father was in authority over her life, and although he had always been very good to her, perhaps she didn't think he'd let her marry Lief Jonason. The man had very little English and he had no profession, no trade above that of a day laborer. But he was a good man and she was happy with him, although life was often hard."

"Did your father send her money?"

"She wouldn't take it. Her husband had pride, in his way. And so had Annie."

"Is it at all possible," Dr. Merrill said, and put his cup down in his saucer, "is it at all possible that underneath the apparent happiness Rafe's mother was actually resentful because she thought she had to run away … because there had been insufficient understanding, which seems to have been on her own part, but which she may have attributed to your father? Is it possible that her husband was bitter because he could not give her what her own people could give? In other words, did this boy Rafe grow up in an atmosphere of very deeply concealed jealousy and resentment?"

Robin got up again and walked to the window. "Me," he said dryly, "I would not care to be a psychologist."

Dr. Merrill looked at him humorously. "Sometimes I don't care much for it myself. Basically, however, I find mystery one of the most satisfying elements of life, and there is nothing more mysterious than personality." He looked at Julie. "Does what I have said make sense, Mrs. Jonason?"

"Not very much," Julie said honestly. "If you read these letters, it is not there, this thing you suggest. Annie's Scottish pride is there. Her anxiety not to make her husband feel less than he was. Her love for him and for the boy. And I have never, never, seen a flicker of this thing in Rafe. Never. Never anything but gratitude to my father for giving him his chance. Gratitude, and affection, and ... love. For all of us."

Robin, at the window, said slowly, "Are you trying to suggest that from the beginning Rafe was playing a part? That his gratitude and affection were assumed? That he has been plotting all along to get control of the Macrae house, as revenge, as a way to show that he himself was big in his own right, bigger than the man who was befriending him, *patronizing* him?"

Dr. Merrill finished his coffee. "You would have been rather good in psychology, perhaps," he decided.

"If that's a possibility," Robin went on, disregarding him, "then it might also be true that Rafe had a personal resentment, born of being weighed and measured, of being watched in those early years. He should have been accepted, perhaps he thought that way. There should have been no period of testing. Surely that's rather unbelievable! Surely no one could expect to walk in and be the son of the house, and such a house, without being tested out!"

"Pathological vanity is very strange. Those who are consumed by it do not conform to social patterns."

Julie felt immeasurably tired, so tired that she knew she would never be rested; and so cold that nothing would ever warm her again. Then the image of her small, laughing, blond baby came into her mind. She let it rest there. She said, "Do you suggest that in all these years, if Rafe truly has been motivated by these terrible emotions, he may have been living out the other part of his life? He said … when he was still unconscious … there were many things he said …"

"I'll tell him," Robin said, and came back to the sofa. He repeated word for word the things Julie had told him. The woman's name … Bess, Bess; the sentence about the wedding ring. The "Bess, I'm already on the train … I'm already on the train."

Merrill listened with the deepest interest, his eyes like pools of light.

When Robin was finished Julie said, "Edie thinks these things go away back to childhood. Do they? Or, has he … is he one of the men who …" She stopped. After a moment she said, "It would break my heart."

Robin said bluntly, "She's had enough, sir. I'll take her home. What do you want us to do?"

"She won't break," Dr. Merrill said mildly, and at his words a sudden warm courage flowed again in Julie's veins. He said again, "Nothing could break her."

"She's been hurt enough."

"Yes."

Julie looked around the room, big and cluttered with books and papers, at Henry Lake writing at the table, at Jonathan Merrill. So much trouble had been in this room, so many problems had been looked at and worked over.

She said suddenly, "I may as well say the worst thing of all. The very worst thing. I know it isn't true, but you'll both be thinking it now. You'll be thinking ... my father, who loved me ... and who trusted Rafe ... you'll be thinking, did Rafe really love me? Did he marry me for love, ugly and ... ugly as I was? Or did my father ... old, and afraid for me ... did my father ... trusting him—did he *buy* him?"

Henry Lake stopped writing. His face was turned toward Julie with sympathy written on it as plainly as if it had been a signboard inscribed in big letters. Robin dropped his head into his hands. But Jonathan Merrill looked at her steadily. "Do you believe that?" he asked.

There were footsteps on the walk outside, the quick twist of the bell, the sound of letters falling through the slot in the front door. Nobody in the room moved.

"How do I know now?" Julie asked.

CHAPTER EIGHT

ON MONDAY AFTERNOON, Julie, after several hours spent in Rafe's office downtown, drove home alone to the house in the village. There was no great pressure yet at the office; the work was well departmentalized, and although most of the men her father had trained were retired now, or dead, Rafe had had a faculty too for training help. But he himself had been such a dynamo and had carried so much of the load that things were beginning to pile up a little, and in any case certain important decisions had waited long enough. He had talked over every aspect of the work with her all their lives, and although she had not his grasp, his vision, she knew fairly well what decisions he would have made if he were able.

Nobody at the office mistrusted him. There was nothing there in the air but utter confidence, and the warmest hope that he would soon be recovered from his accident and able to come to work. Nobody knew, not even his secretary, Mary Goodman, who had been Hugh Macrae's secretary for years, that there was anything wrong with him now except weakness and an incomplete recovery from the long unconsciousness.

Well ... was there?

Julie turned her car into the wide drive and went on to the back of the house. As she reached the garage doors their new man, who was Henry Lake, came from the back of the house. He wore a neat dark uniform, a chauffeur's livery. He had been in the house since Saturday. He slept in the room next to Rafe's; he was ostensibly a servant, a man filling in while Rafe was ill, taking care of the cars, doing the shopping for Jennie, taking Nellie and Hugh out driving, caring for the garden, washing windows and keeping the basement in order. He was wonderful. His coming was something decided on by Jonathan Merrill and Robin. He was much needed, had always been needed, Julie realized, and had already decided that when this bad time was over she would find a man to do the things Henry Lake did, to relieve Rafe of a considerable load. Not that Rafe did the actual work of cleaning cars, and raking leaves, and shoveling snow in winter, but he saw that it was done and took charge of the doing. This was the sort of simple living that her father had believed in. There was a place here for a good man; she should have seen it long ago, Julie decided, and reproached herself. Rafe had been doing far too much.

Could you have a nervous breakdown from overwork and disintegrate as Rafe had done? Did that happen? Could it happen? Overwork, and a bad shock? Would that change a personality?

Henry Lake held the door open and she got out. "Thank you, Henry. Is everything all right?"

He looked down at her. He had such a nice face, steady but sensitive, kind but not soft. "Nellie is out walking with the boy," he answered. "They have been gone an hour and three quarters. Miss Macrae had a dental appointment for four o'clock at the Medical Arts Building and she took her own car, Mrs. Jonason. As for Mr. Jonason …"

"Yes?"

"I have to report that he is dressed and downstairs. He came down shortly after you had gone, and he told Miss Macrae with some decision that he was now through with staying in bed, that he had dismissed the nurse, whether the doctor agreed or not."

Julie opened the clasp of her bag and shut it again. "Was he angry?"

"Just firm, Mrs. Jonason. Almost normal, I should say. That is, a man in his senses might come to exactly his decision at a certain point in his convalescence."

"You hadn't seen him before, Henry?"

"No." He walked to the front of the car, bent and examined a tire, came back and pointed to it. Julie's eyes followed his finger, puzzled. "There is nothing wrong with the tire," he said. "But Mr. Jonason is watching from behind the dining room curtain."

"I see," Julie murmured. She, too, walked toward the front of the car. She looked down at the tire and nodded. She turned toward the house. "Jennie and Nellie take you at face value," she murmured. "They think a manservant is a fine thing, so we are quite safe there."

"Yes, madam," he said. He slid in behind the wheel of the car and drove it into the garage. Julie went on to the house, in at the side door, and on upstairs to her room. She stood for a moment at the mirror there, her hand pressed to her wildly beating heart. The color was high in her cheeks. She took off her gloves and pressed her fingers against the spots of heat. She looked frightened. It would not do, to look frightened.

When she was calmer she took off the swinging brown coat and hung it carefully in her dressing-room closet. She put her purse and gloves in the drawer. She came back to the mirror and took up the comb, to part her hair neatly in the middle and brush it down a little. She pushed the narrow combs in on either side. She looked quite calm again. Neat and quiet and calm. She was wearing a brown knitted dress today, one Edie had made, that looked well on her slimness. She went into the bathroom and washed her hands, and then shut her room door steadily behind herself and went downstairs.

Rafe was not in the hall. He was not in the living room. Her heart began to pound again. She walked through the empty dining room and on out to the kitchen. Jennie was there, humming to herself and rolling out piecrust. Her round face was bright and cheerful. She looked up and said, "I heard the car come in, Miss Julie. It's nice to have that good man around to take care of it for you. We've needed him or his like for a long time." She smiled. "I'm making butter tarts. It's good to have men to cook for. I suppose you know that nurse is gone, and Mr. Jonason's downstairs, for good, he says?"

"Henry told me. Where is he, Jennie?"

"He's in the study. Maybe he's laying down. You know, he doesn't seem right to me yet, not by a long way. He's thin, and he's not too strong on his pins, but I don't think his head's acting right yet either. He's still wandering a bit."

"What did he say?"

"Oh, nothing. He come out here and I started to talk to him, the way I always did, but he didn't joke. I didn't really expect him to," Jennie admitted. "He's been too sick. But he just looked blank, like, and said it was a nice day, or something, and backed out."

"Jennie … he hasn't got all his memory back. It's patchy. It … it may take quite a while. We'll have to help him and be patient."

"Well, bless your heart," Jennie said comfortably. "I won't pay no attention. My nephew come back from the war, with some kind of a knock on the head, maybe not even as bad as Mr. Jonason, and he didn't know his own mother for six months. It takes everybody different. As you say, it's just help him and be patient, and one day he'll come out of it, right as rain."

Julie went out of the kitchen again and into the hall. On the other side of it, the study door at the foot of the stairs was closed. She stood looking at it for a long time.

While she was standing there Henry Lake came into the hall from the kitchen door. He took a folded paper from his pocket, then turned and walked into the dining room. Julie followed. She shut the door after her.

He handed her the paper, unfolded. It was a half sheet of bond, and on it was typed:

FINGERPRINTS: From yesterday's glass off breakfast tray; from electric razor kept in Jonason's office washroom; from silver pen box in locked drawer of Macrae house desk (opened only with Jonason's own keys) *identical*.

TEETH: From impression made Saturday morning while subject still deeply asleep, impression compared with Dr. Howard White's office records; the same.

This man is Rafe Jonason.

It was initialed J.M.

Julie read the paper over and over. She leaned against the wall and looked at it through a blur of tears. She wiped her eyes with the back of her wrist. She read the paper again and gave it back to Henry Lake.

He said under his breath, "There has been no substitution."

"Does Mr. Sloan know?"

"With your permission, I shall telephone him. This was just delivered by special messenger to me."

She whispered, "I don't know whether this is good or bad. I haven't seen him. I'm afraid to see him. Maybe he has changed."

"I think not."

She looked up at him quickly.

"May I make a suggestion, Mrs. Jonason?"

"Of course, of course!"

"Mr. Sloan told Dr. Merrill and myself last night, in a further interview at Dr. Merrill's office, that Mr. Jonason had said several times that he knew who he was. He wasn't Rafe Jonason; but he knew who he was."

"Yes. He said that."

"Dr. Merrill thinks it would be extremely good if we could find out who he thinks he is."

Julie said, "It's only insane people who think they're someone else. Insane people!"

"There are one or two other possibilities in Dr. Merrill's mind. He is not inclined to insanity as such."

"I don't see what other possibilities there could be!"

"Perhaps he will talk to you, Mrs. Jonason."

Julie turned and went back into the big hall. She sat down on the long velvet-covered settle beside the fireplace. After a while she was calmer. It was Rafe who was in the study; there was no longer any doubt. The most clever imposter could not manage to produce all this irrefutable proof. So it was Rafe she must deal with, and he was ill. That was what she had to keep remembering. Ill.

She got up and went steadily to the study door. She opened it.

He was there, sitting at the big desk as he had so often sat, an elbow on the desk, his head propped in his hand. As she entered he looked up. He rose. He *was* Rafe! He was, he was!

She said, "They tell me you've decided against nurses and beds, darling."

His eyelids flickered. "I have decided against nurses and beds. Yes."

She sat down on the red-leather sofa. "How do you feel?"

"I feel fine. Like something in a cage, but fine." His eyes never left her face.

He was thin. There were dark circles under his eyes. His cheeks were almost as hollow as Jonathan Merrill's. His clothes hung on him.

"There is no cage."

"That's what you tell me," he said. "Suppose I walked out of here … put on my hat and coat and walked out of here. What would happen?"

"I wish you wouldn't think of it, Rafe. You're not well yet, dear. You're really not well."

His mouth tightened. His voice was still harsh, bitter. "I am perfectly well."

"Where do you want to go?"

"How can I go anywhere? There is no money in my wallet. It isn't even my wallet. I had ..." He stopped. He sat down again and put his head in his hands. "My God," he said. He looked up. "What year is this?"

Julie got up and went across to him. She lifted the small metal calendar from the corner of the desk, and put it before him. He stared at it in something like horror. After a long time he looked up at her. "I guess I'm crazy," he said. "I guess that's it."

"Many people lose their memories for a time, Rafe. Many people. Don't they call it amnesia? It will come back to you. Truly, it will. Some little thing will happen and suddenly it will all be clear. The past you do remember ... whatever that is ... and the years you've lost, they will join together again."

"Is that was the doctor orders?"

"It's what he says happens."

"What doctor? The old grandmother who was yapping here the other night?"

Julie thought, dear God ... he's speaking the language of his youth, the language he heard when he was a child, rough talk, the talk of rough people. That's all this is. That's all it can be.

Better not mention any other doctor. Not Jonathan Merrill, as a psychologist.

"Dr. Prescott has always been our doctor," she said. She went back to the sofa. She curled up in the corner, making herself small. He got up from behind the desk and came to sit in a chair near her. He looked at her evenly.

"I wouldn't have married you, that's one thing," he said. "That's one sure thing. You're a damned pretty girl, but I wouldn't have married you. You're not the kind I go for. You're little and scared and soft and easy. I never did like that kind of woman. I like them with guts."

After a moment Julie said, "Do you? What color guts, blonde or brunette?"

"Well," he said. He laughed. "Well. Maybe I misjudged you."

"Maybe you did. And … since you are so critical of who and what we say you are now, perhaps you'll tell me who you really are that's so much better? Or do you know? Or are you bluffing? I imagine you are. Bluffing."

His eyes, blue and frosty, were suddenly veiled. He smiled. "*Who* is bluffing?" he inquired. "Who told you to see if you could find out who I am? Who told you?"

The front door opened. Julie had left the study door wide. In through the front door, into the hall, little Hugh trotted, followed by plump Nellie. She caught him there in the middle of the hall, knelt down, and pulled off his white helmet, his white coat with the dark blue collar. He emerged rosy and laughing in a bright-coral knitted suit. The color in his cheeks matched the suit exactly. He was beautiful, with the soft curling fair hair, the sparkling blue of his eyes, the white skin painted with coral lips and cheeks.

Rafe had seen him. He was staring at him, dazed, bewildered.

Julie turned. She called, "Hughie, darling. Mommy's here."

Rafe shot her a horrified glance. He did not speak.

The baby saw her. He began to run toward her in his staggering baby eagerness. He held out his arms, laughing. "Mommy, mommy," he said cheerfully. "Mommy, mommy."

She knelt down and caught him in her arms. He gave her wet kisses and patted her face. She hugged him. She turned with him to Rafe, who was on his feet, his eyes unbelieving.

Hugh saw him. There was a second of hesitation, then he put out his small arms and said joyfully, "Dada! Dada!"

Julie moved and held the baby out to Rafe, whose arms moved automatically. Hughie flung his arms around his father's neck and patted his face too, full of joy and love.

Rafe's eyes searched Julie's, the eyes of a distracted creature, driven and distracted.

"If you don't believe he is your son," Julie said evenly, "carry him over there and look in the mirror."

CHAPTER NINE

THE DINNER TABLE was pleasant, the long stretch of rubbed oak set with the place mats of brown heavy lace with the low bowl of yellow roses in the center and tall yellow candles in the branched holders flanking the roses. Julie sat in her usual place nearest the pantry door, and they had put Rafe at the head of the table where he had always sat. On Rafe's right was Mrs. Prescott, and beside her Robin; across the table, Edie and Dr. Prescott sat facing the sideboard, gleaming in the candlelight with the heavy silver Hugh Macrae had collected almost with passion; the immense tray standing against the wall of the shallow alcove in which the sideboard stood, the two silver punch bowls, one at either end of the tray, the cups, the ice pitcher, the row of silver goblets. The pieces were not just for show but often used; Rafe had loved parties, and there had been many since Julie's face had been made well, big buffet suppers with all the specialties of the house set out lavishly, the best food, the best drink. Served with dignity and pride and color and warmth. This was a lovely house for such parties; when the hall fire was lit, the hearth in the study glowing, the living-room fireplace adding its warmth and brightness; when there were bowls of flowers everywhere, when the hidden record player in the hall whispered soft music that threaded its way in and out of conversations and the rooms were filled with interesting people, Rafe had been at his happiest.

Julie glanced down the table. This Rafe tonight was anything but happy. His face was tense and pale, and he glanced at his guests as if he feared them.

His first sight of the baby, yesterday afternoon, had made in him a great change. He was more confused than ever, but less belligerent. The baby was his very image; he had stood before the mirror, holding the little boy, for long minutes, staring from one set of brilliant blue eyes to the other; eyes set at that faint tip-tilted angle in the head, with the thick lashes in the outer corners; at the pale, pale blond hair, growing identically from the forehead in a square, definite line; at the fine ears, faintly pointed and very flat to the head; at the curve of the mouth. The noses were identical, straight and not too long, finely made; and the cleft in the small chin, so marked in a baby, was the cleft in Rafe's own chin. The child was his, and he knew it; and the knowledge had brought about in him a conviction that it was he who was wrong; that he was not being forced into a situation that was not his own, that the things all of them said—Julie, Robin, Edie, Dr. Prescott— these things were true.

But they obviously didn't fit in with whatever it was he believed of himself: the picture he had in his mind, the memories, the conception of himself.

Mrs. Prescott was saying in her warm, gentle way, "It's so nice to have Rafe well again. We were all so *worried,* Rafe. You had such a terrible accident. Nat really walked the floor over you, and he's stopped doing that about most people, long ago."

Rafe looked at her and said flatly, "Very kind of him."

Henry Lake came in with the roast on its big silver platter. He set it down in front of Rafe, who leaned back in his chair and looked at it as if he had never seen a roast of beef before. Henry lifted the carving knife and fork from their small stands beside the platter and laid them ready, one on each side of the meat.

"Doesn't that look wonderful!" Mrs. Prescott said.

Both Robin and Edie were watching Rafe, carefully casual. Henry Lake went out in his white coat and came in again, to set the silver vegetable dishes before Julie. He took the lids off. He brought in the plates.

Rafe lifted his eyes and looked down the table at Julie. His glance was pure hatred. He took a breath. He said, "Tell the man to take this back to the kitchen, will you, and carve it there? I don't feel exactly up to it."

Julie glanced at Henry Lake. He lifted the platter and carried it away.

Mrs. Prescott put out a plump hand and patted Rafe's as it lay on the table. "Poor boy," she said gently. "I imagine you'll feel shaky for a long, long time."

It was Dr. Prescott who brought openness into the situation. He said, "What seems to have happened, my boy, is that you have forgotten all the things you have learned in the past eighteen years. Don't be concerned about it. We may as well face it. It's the normal pattern of amnesia. Many, many people have suffered from it."

Rafe looked at him, listening. At her end of the table, Julie found herself praying to herself. Dear God, let him listen. Dear God, don't let him shut himself away and be alone.

Dr. Prescott leaned forward, his fine strong hands linked at the edge of the table. "When you came here, you were only eighteen," he said.

"I was twenty-one."

"No, no," Dr. Prescott said. "You were eighteen. I don't know why you think you were twenty-one. You weren't. You brought your birth certificate, although of course we all knew exactly when Annie's boy was born. But Hugh hadn't seen you since you were a small lad, and he had asked you to bring it, I suppose as legal proof of your identity, not that he had any real doubt. You strongly resemble your father. Your features are a bit finer, your bones are not so large, you are taller; but the coloring is the same, and the set of the head."

Rafe was watching him intently. "So I brought my birth certificate."

"Yes, and the letters Hugh and Edie, here, had written to your mother. And a few other odd papers ... as I remember it, your mother's marriage certificate, and your father's papers from Iceland. You were not, actually, a Canadian citizen, and one of the first things you and Hugh did was to set about acquiring your Canadian papers." He looked up inquiringly. "This is all Greek to you, I take it?"

"There's no sense in a word of it. I'm not ... I don't ... If I do remember anything, it's ... it doesn't ..." He stopped.

Henry Lake brought the meat back, beautifully sliced, and set the platter before Rafe. He stood waiting. Rafe glanced up at him.

Julie said easily, "Mrs. Prescott likes the well-done part, dear. That nice slice on your right would just suit her."

He lifted the fork with its horn handle and took up the slice of meat with it. He put it on the top plate. Henry Lake lifted it and brought it to Julie. She put the broccoli and the parsnips and the browned potatoes on the plate, and Henry carried it back to Mrs. Prescott.

"And Edie likes hers medium rare," Julie said.

Mrs. Prescott was looking at Rafe in blank questioning. She glanced at her husband. He shook his head very faintly. She turned over the new ideas in her mind. She straightened the pearls at her plump throat and settled back in her chair. She smiled at Julie.

The serving was managed. The hollandaise in its silver dish was passed. Henry filled the water goblets again. Julie lifted her fork.

Rafe ate awkwardly. He was much more awkward than he had been during that very first meal together, when he had first come. Julie remembered that first meal so well, because she herself, bitterly self-conscious in the presence of a stranger, had watched him with the deepest awareness. He had been slow then, waiting for Edie and for Julie's father to show what to do; he had been open and honest about his unfamiliarity with social customs. This house had always been simple, with the food served by host and hostess at table, but Rafe had, he had told them then, never eaten anywhere except at the long tables of the lumbering camps, with the men reaching across each other for the dishes of hot food, with no politeness, no pretences at anything but hunger. His honesty about his lack of knowledge had been the second thing to win her father's heart. Rafe had soon learned to eat nicely.

He learned now, again.

What *is this,* Julie said inside herself, what *is* this? He is not even the boy who came here; he is *someone else.*

But he was not someone else. He was the same boy. He was Rafe.

Edie did not believe it. Nothing had convinced her; not Dr. Prescott's certainty, not Jonathan Merrill's proof of fingerprints and teeth, nothing. This was not Rafe.

She had said to Julie last night, when they were in the baby's room together, "Juliet, you'll not let that man in your room. You'll not let him go to bed with you."

And Julie, her heart sick, had said, "He won't come. I don't want him, Edie. But even if I did ... he hates me. He won't come." And then in the back of her mind, she heard him saying again "Bess ... Bess."

On the telephone today Jonathan Merrill had said, "Don't press him. Don't question him. But don't miss a word. This is indeed a mystery."

Henry Lake had a notebook in the pantry. Everything went into it.

Robin, familiar and comforting there beside Julie, was not content with patience which stretched out ahead of them with no end. He had his own theories about how Rafe should be handled, in spite of his faith and trust in Jonathan Merrill. It was his determination to try out those theories which brought about a minor crisis at dinner. They were nearly through; the meat and vegetables had been taken away, the small salad eaten and the plates

89

removed, and the dessert, of pears baked in honey and some of Jennie's best nutcake, was almost finished. Rafe was managing very well, even conversing a little with Mrs. Prescott, who had taken her cue and confined herself to the weather, the food, the intricate tracery of the old silver platter; and Edie had got herself under control so that her whole manner did not bristle. Dr. Prescott was thoughtful, but his calmness suggested that he had no doubts or fears. Robin was not calm.

He finished his dessert and laid down his fork and spoon. He leaned his elbows on the table, crossed his arms, and looked at Rafe. He said, "You know, old man, you did considerable talking when you were coming out from under this concussion of yours."

Rafe looked at him, startled. His face, almost pleasant a moment before, stiffened and went blank. "Is that so?" he replied. He didn't seem to like Robin very much. But he made an effort. It was as if his meeting with little Hugh last night had made him understand that he must make an effort. "Did I say anything that might give us a clue as to where my thinking apparatus sprang a leak?" he asked.

"Well, we don't know," Robin answered. "The things you said don't make any sense to any of us. You talked about a wedding ring, for instance."

Rafe lifted an eyebrow. "Not very suggestive of anything, is it? The world's full of wedding rings." He glanced down the table. "Julie's got one, and a very nice one. I suppose I bought it. I think I have good taste."

"Hers is a valuable ring and beautiful. But you said, 'Not much of a wedding ring,' you see. As if you were scornful. Does that ring a bell?"

Rafe's eyes, fixed on his, did not flicker. "A completely meaningless remark."

"It seemed so."

Under the table, Julie found Robin's toe and gave it a small warning kick. But he drew his foot away.

"You also talked about someone named Bess," Robin went on. "There doesn't seem to have been any Bess in your youth. I suppose that doesn't ring a bell either."

Rafe smiled, an easy smile. He shook his head. "Maybe I read a book when I was young," he said. "Wasn't there a landlord's daughter named Bess? Seems to me I have a picture of her leaning out of a window."

"Oh," Mrs. Prescott said happily, "that's 'The Highwayman.' Alfred Noyes. You know ... 'and Bess, the landlord's daughter ... the landlord's black-eyed daughter' ... you know, who was in love with this robber, this highwayman—of course in those days it wasn't stealing, in a way, I mean, the men who did it were practically heroes—he wore a red velvet coat, didn't he? 'The wind was a torrent of darkness, among the dusty trees' ... my word, I think I could remember it if I had to...."

Julie said quickly, "Rafe knows it all. I remember now. He used to declaim it with gestures." Her eyes filled suddenly with tears. Her heart warmed again. She laughed. "I'd forgotten all about that Bess. It was because I was thinking of a *blonde* Bess, I guess."

Rafe's level eyes came to her face. "A blonde Bess?" He moved the spoon on his empty plate. "Why blonde?"

"Oh," Julie said confusedly, "Like Miss Burnell. You called her Bess, you see."

"Yes, I see," he said evenly. He looked at Robin. "And what else did I confess while I didn't know what I was doing? What else?"

Robin regarded him thoughtfully. "Well, nothing else, Rafe. I wasn't trying to put you on the spot. Helping you to remember, that's all."

"What else did I say?"

"There was just one more sensible thing," Julie said quickly. "The little bit about the train. That's all."

His face whitened. His eyes looked like blue, angry fire. But his voice was quiet. "And what did I say about a train?"

91

Henry Lake came in and began to take the dessert plates. He did not look at Julie. She crumpled her napkin in her hand. She said, "It was I who heard you, darling. All you said was … 'Bess, Bess, I'm on the train already! Look, I'm on the train already.'"

His burning eyes held hers. She could feel the tears again behind her lashes. She glanced round the table and rose. "It wasn't anything of importance, Rafe. Edie says you were five years old again and playing train with some child. I'm … sorry it doesn't help."

He got up too, still looking at her, and stood, tall and white-faced, at the other end of the table. He got hold of himself at last. He looked at Edie, the first look he had given her. He said pleasantly, with ice beneath the pleasantness, "Thank you very much, Edie. I'm sure that's the explanation. You're very smart to figure it out."

CHAPTER TEN

AT NINE-THIRTY on the evening of the dinner party, while the guests were still in the Macrae house, sitting in the study listening—of all things—to Handel's *Messiah*, all thirty-three records of it, Police Constable Henry Lake went out of the house, caught the Bay subway, and went down to report to his chief, Dr. Jonathan Merrill. All the way down in the subway he sat motionless. A trio of girls with badminton rackets got on at the corner of St. Clair and Yonge, and his mind automatically mentioned "Granite Club," sorted the girls out, noted their clothes, the thick legs of one, the two class pins flaunted on another, the oddly meek but brilliant thin face of the third, and he knew that a month from now he could if necessary—which was certainly unlikely—write a minutely detailed description of all three of them. By that time, the mind being what it was, working away all the time on a subterranean level, he would probably be able to put names to them. If they were Granite Club, they were Society. One would perhaps have a sister marrying and her picture would be in the paper, the sister's, and this girl would be somewhere in the wedding group, even the thick-legged one. Her name would fix her in a certain social group. She would go to school to Bishop Strachan, or Havergal, or Loretto Abbey.

P.C. Lake drew himself up sharply. He was not interested in these girls.

Still, *two* class pins ... he could make out one. Camberwell College. A cramming school for the sons of the very rich, either the not very bright sons or the bad ones. The other was a fraternity pin. This child, not more than sixteen, had a university frat pin and a pin from Camberwell. He made out which fraternity the pin belonged to, finally.

As for the meek little thing with the brilliant eyes ... she had a long scar running across her throat, as if she might have had a goiter operation ... at her age? ... or a cut ... queer place for a cut ... throat ...

Two years ago the little daughter of Gilbert Bolsover-Royden had tried to kill herself because her father had re-married and she had hated the stepmother.

Well, it was all clear enough. Bolsover-Royden had a wild son, eighteen years old, who drove a white convertible and had arrived at Camberwell, having been dismissed from every other school in Toronto. The other girl, the pretty one, was wearing his pin, and playing badminton with his sister. Granite Club ... Camberwell ... Bolsover-Royden ...

They got up, still giggling and casting flirtatious glances in his direction—thick legs and class pins, anyway—and got off at Wellesley. This was the connection for the Rosedale bus. Thick legs had a proprietary air; she was being hostess. So she lived in Rosedale and was taking Bolsover-Royden and class pins home with her. She was arrogant. She was proud. It must be purse-proud; she had nothing else.

Well ... Rosedale ... old families ... and Bolsover-Royden was a snob ... so who ... Granite Club, Bolsover-Royden ... Camberwell, Rosedale, old families, money, and probably Havergal. So who ...

Police Constable Lake got up abruptly and mentally shook himself. The car had arrived at College Street. He went along to headquarters, spent half an hour there, and then took a taxi north. He arrived shortly at Dr. Merrill's house. He went up the walk and opened the door of the office with his key. He went in.

Jonathan Merrill was there. He was always there. He went into the main house and went to bed about four o'clock in the morning, usually, and slept then until ten or so. If he slept. There was some doubt in P.C. Lake's mind about the sleeping, because apparently there was never any time off in Dr. Merrill's thinking. He went to bed with an unsolved problem and he got up with the answer. He lived on black coffee and cigarettes and he had no personal life to speak of, no physical life anyway. He didn't play games or go for walks or indulge in feminine company. He was not married. He was warm, human, sympathetic, but in a way exceedingly remote. Still, he did have his sister, Jane. They were very close, in an odd unspeaking way. She was with him now. She was in the room, anyway, sitting in the small armchair beyond Jonathan Merrill's desk, her sketch pad on a pastry board on her knee, her hand busy with a heavy black pencil. She was a small girl, and good to look at, with bright warmth in her face, a very pleasant contour which was more or less out of bounds in P.C. Lake's thinking, and extremely pleasant ankles, which were also out of bounds but so charming that a man might well consider them simply an artistic exercise and admire them as such.

She looked up at the sound of his entrance. "Hi, Henry," she said happily. "I was hoping you might come."

Her brother looked at her. "I mentioned that he was coming."

"Oh, no, you didn't," Jane Merrill said. "Not out loud. Not to me, angel." She was not perturbed. She was accustomed to her brother. She accepted him.

He laid down his pen. He reached for the box of cigarettes beyond his telephone. He gave Henry one of his quick glances. He never looked at anyone for very long. It was as if he saw as much as he needed in one of those half looks.

Henry closed the hall door behind him. He went across the room and sat down on one of the straight chairs drawn up to the desk at which Jonathan Merrill was working. This was the general desk. The other two tables of the three pushed together were specialized. The far one was for police work. It looked fairly clear. The one nearest the door was University of Toronto psychology, a row of reference books separating it from the others, a stack of psychological journals, new texts, reports, students' theses, in neat piles over its surface. The general desk might hold anything.

Jane looked at him with her charming smile. "How do you like being a houseman, Henry?"

"It's very interesting," Henry replied. He looked at Jonathan Merrill. "Sir, what family living in Rosedale would be intimate with the Bolsover-Roydens? A family allowing the daughters such latitude as riding on the subway?"

"Mmm."

Jane looked from one man to the other. Jonathan Merrill picked up the pen again and made a squiggle on his paper. He said, "The Greenings? Five children. Greening holds a considerable interest in Bolsover-Royden's pulp mills."

Jane's eyes were interested. "A sixteen-year-old girl?"

"I should imagine so."

"A hoydenish girl," Jane said thoughtfully. "Her mother's despair. She is fat and homely and hoydenish and hasn't a hope."

P.C. Lake nodded. He relaxed.

"Would she have anything to do with anything?" Jane asked politely.

"No, nothing."

"Well, that's good," Jane said. She got up and put her sketch, tacked to the pastry board, inside the door to the main house. She came back and sat down. She folded her clever small hands in her lap and waited. Jane was very good at waiting. She was very good at everything.

Henry Lake got out his notebook. He opened the pages on their rings and laid them flat.

Jonathan Merrill reached forward, crushed out his cigarette, and lit another.

Henry Lake said, "It would seem that Rafe Jonason is in serious need of psychiatric help."

Merrill said mildly, "He is insane?"

"He is aware of being two men. I think he is aware of being *three* men."

"Yes," Jonathan Merrill murmured. "Yes."

"The man the Macraes and everyone else tell him he is. The man he was, the boy, rather, before he came east. And someone else. That is, there are three lives inside his head and he doesn't know which are real. Two of them have to be real; a youth and a manhood. He is accepting now that he is being told the truth about his life since he came to Toronto. He has the outer facts straight about that life. He has asked many questions about the business, about the work he has done, about the physical facts ... Hugh Macrae's death, how and where and when it took place, for instance."

Jonathan Merrill said slowly, "Macrae died of a heart attack on a hunting trip."

"Yes," P.C. Lake said thoughtfully. "Miss Edith Macrae may have been carrying secret, perhaps unrecognized resentment toward Jonason ever since that time, although he did all he could. There was nothing any man could have done. Macrae had an attack of angina. He had never had angina before. The two men were alone up in Haliburton. Jonason took care of him, nursed him for a day and a night, not daring to leave him. There was no help within thirty miles, and the guide was not due back for two days. When he came, Macrae was dead. They got him out to the doctor at Huntsville, who heard the story and assured Jonason there was nothing he could have done. But Miss Macrae idolized her brother and it may be that some of her extra resentment against Jonason now is a carry-over, unrecognized, of her resentment toward Jonason at that time. She is being far more difficult now than anyone else, far worse than his wife. She knows this man is Rafe

Jonason, she realizes he has been very ill, but she will not accept him. Yet they say she was very fond of him always. It looked to be a sincere fondness, and never failed except just after her brother's death, when she felt that surely Jonason might have got Macrae out of there and to a doctor in time. But the man was helpless, they were in a trackless wilderness."

"I can see that," Jane said. "It's reasonable. She probably thinks if she'd been there she'd have done better. She's never married, maybe she hadn't a very high opinion of men really. Maybe she never truly believed in any man but her own brother."

Her brother turned and gave her one of his rare smiles. "You raid my bookshelf," he said.

"I listen to your brilliant conversation," she answered tartly. "You have to remember that I've been letting the waves of psychology wash over me since I was about two. And after all, my sweet, I adore you. I have the same feeling for my brother that Edith Macrae has for hers. That's why I, at twenty-four, have never married. I shall never marry. I shall never find a man so …"

"Women who talk never find any men," Jonathan Merrill remarked. He turned back to Henry. "Miss Macrae is not happy about Mr. Jonason."

"She is very unhappy. She talks of nothing else. She has had long talks with Dr. Prescott, with Mr. Sloan, and with me. She watches her niece every second. She is constantly overcome with this man's resemblance to Jonason but as constantly disconcerted by his personality difference. Apparently it is very marked. Jonason was always kind, always thoughtful, always polite, mannerly, gentle, affectionate. He never said a cross word. He never lost his temper. He was extremely patient, had great foresight, understood other people's feelings, never made the smallest error. He gave the right amount of money to charity, he supported the church, he did everything just right. In fact," Henry Lake ended, "he was a paragon of all the virtues."

Jane said dryly, "It just ain't so. The mold's busted."

"A pattern emerges." Henry Lake agreed.

"His wife?"

Henry Lake stirred in his chair. Julie's face was always in his mind; it was a lovely face, a deeply compassionate face, its soft mouth tender and hopeful, the eyes shadowed and darkly aware of pain. She had too many fears to meet life easily; she had leaned strongly on her husband.

He said, "She is having a difficult time. She is a … well, she is a spiritual person. She could not love the man Jonason is now; he is hard, bitter, selfish, often cruel; I would say that he has frequently given indications of a basic viciousness such as she has never encountered. She wants to love him; she has the most tremendous gratitude toward him for what he did for her from the beginning, making her feel human. She had been an outcast. And they were obviously more than happy." He stopped. "Their marriage was the sort of thing marriage ought to be. They were one. But she could not be one with this man, even if he wanted it, and as the days go by, in spite of her trying, she is drawing further away."

"It may be a good thing."

"She will be stronger for it, eventually. More able in herself. But the cleavage is very painful to her, and very bewildering."

"Sloan?"

"He is a good man, sir. No paragon. But a good, sound, honest man. Also of course he is in love with Mrs. Jonason. But it seems that no word or sign of this has escaped him, and although Miss Macrae is aware of it, Mrs. Jonason seems not to be." He paused. "This deep concern for her has impelled him on a few occasions to goad Jonason a little. I doubt if he really grasps what is going on in the man's mind."

After a time Jonathan Merrill said, "I don't know that we ever had a nicer problem." He rubbed an eyebrow thoughtfully. "You think that Jonason finds it not only difficult to accept what they tell him he has been and done since he came east, but that the facts of his boyhood are strange too?"

"I am sure of it, sir. Nothing rings a bell. No mention of his mother, his father, his childhood in the lumber camps ... nothing."

"But he has other memories?"

"I am sure he has the image of another life in his mind." Henry Lake laid the notebook down and recounted the scene at tonight's dinner, the repeating by Robin Sloan of Jonason's words in hospital and Jonason's white-faced, angry—well, frightened—reception of them.

At the end, Jane said, "He *is* another man. In his own mind. Isn't that clear? There's a whole life there, with a Bess in it, as plain as day ... a life that ended years ago, when he was young. Jon, a person can invent such a life ... I mean, the boy was undoubtedly lonely when he was little. Lonely and deprived. Children do invent lives and playmates, and give them names and reality. This boy was bright, imaginative. Must have been, or he wouldn't have been so successful in this new life. Could he have invented a whole life for himself ... and maybe, all these years when he's been such a paragon, little bits got added to it? He must have felt insecure plenty of times in this place. Couldn't he have been carrying around another world in which he didn't have to feel insecure?" She got up and went and poked the smoldering fire. It broke into a quick vibrancy. She turned. Her eyes were thoughtful. "Look ... his Julie is small and dark-haired and fearful, needing protection. *He* needs protection too, in a way. He isn't the big confident man they need him to be, not really. How *could* he be, with no background, no education, no social experience? So he keeps building on to the life he'd begun for himself … you say this nurse he called Bess, who reminded him of the Bess in his mind, was a tall blonde. Of course, someone the opposite of Julie. He probably loved Julie to death, but she *needed* him too much. The pressure got too heavy. Jon, darling, my erudite and all-knowing brother, am I talking sense?"

Henry Lake was watching her in complete admiration. She caught his glance. But she wasn't thinking about him. She never thought about him.

Her brother said honestly, "I am often quite overcome by the depth of your insight."

The flames leaped up in the little corner fireplace. Jane said abruptly, "That's my swan song. I will now make coffee. Henry, could you eat a sandwich? I have some elegant venison, believe it or not. Last year's, out of the freezer. I thought we'd better eat it before people go hunting next month and bring us a lot more. I could make you a delicious venison sandwich. Do housemen get anything to eat?"

"Not venison, Miss Merrill."

She shot him a quick, enigmatic glance at the "Miss Merrill" and vanished.

Jonathan Merrill was examining his fingertips critically. They seemed to be intact. After a time he said absently, "Exactly when did Rafe Jonason come to Toronto?"

"Eighteen years and four months ago, sir. On the twenty-ninth of April, he arrived. It was Juliet Macrae's birthday, her fifteenth birthday. She had a new blue dress—they call it Elizabeth blue now—and she had her hair tied back with a blue ribbon to match. It has always been very pretty hair. She came down the stairs and he was standing in the hall, and he looked up and saw her."

"Miss Edith Macrae?"

"She has a remarkable memory for detail."

"How did he come? By train?"

Henry Lake looked at him. He said slowly, "By train, sir, right."

"Macrae had sent him money?"

"Five hundred dollars, sir. In cash, by registered mail. There was not even a bank in the northern community in which the boy was. He gathered together the letters we spoke of, a very few possessions, went down to Vancouver (I gather by a coastal lumber carrier), bought a new suit of clothes, and then got on the train and came on east."

"Had he money left when he got here?"

"Yes, sir. He spent very little over and above the clothes and his train ticket. He had not visited the diner. He had eaten sandwiches at the various train stops. It was not what Hugh Macrae had intended, but his Scottish thrift was pleased that the boy, with five hundred dollars to spend, should have brought so much back and offered to return it."

"Did Macrae accept it?"

"No. Jonason was told to begin his own private savings account with it. He did."

Jonathan Merrill moved his ash tray three inches to the right and three inches to the left again. He pushed the thin long fingers of his right hand into his hair. "Have you heard anything about his bank balance, does anybody know what he owns in his own right in the way of money, or how he has spent it?"

"I have heard nothing." Henry Lake made a note to himself on his book.

"Henry."

"Sir?"

"Find out if he came Canadian National or Canadian Pacific. Find out when his train left Vancouver. Go back to the railway records and look up that very train ... see if anything happened. See if there was a wreck; see if anything occurred that might have given this backwoods youngster a shock. Any sort of shock. See if there was anything different about that train. It's a forlorn hope ... it would have to be something remarkable to have been kept in the records all this time. Check back on the timing ... read the newspapers of Vancouver for those days ... the papers here. What was going on in the world in those days? We were coming to the end of the depression. April twenty-ninth, 1937, when he got here. I think it takes about four days. The twenty-fifth of April, 1937. Something about a train bothers him. See if it was *that* train, Henry."

"Yes, sir," Henry Lake said. He made another note in his book.

Jane Merrill came back with the sandwiches.

CHAPTER ELEVEN

IT WAS MIDNIGHT. Julie sat curled in the wide soft, blue chair in her bedroom alcove, trying to read a book she had brought home today from the library, trying to read it and understand it. There were three others from the same library shelf piled on the table under the reading lamp. She had come upstairs and seen to the baby, taken him up, cuddled him, changed his diaper, and tucked him in again; then she had taken a bath and got into a ruffled white nylon nightgown and the full, soft, nylon robe, heavy with lace, that matched. The house was warm.

She rubbed her forehead. She read, "Memory, of course, enters as an intrinsic element in these manifestations just as it is an intrinsic element in all thought. The automatic script that describes the memories of a long-forgotten childhood experience may at the same time reason, indulge in jests, rhyme, express cogitation and understanding of questions—indeed (if put to the test) might not only pass a Binet-Simon examination for intelligence, but take a high rank in a Civil Service examination. In these more elaborate exhibitions of subconscious intelligence it is obvious that there is an exuberant efflorescence of the residua deposited in many unconscious fields by life's experiences, and synthesized into a *subconscious functioning system.*"

She took a long breath and shut her eyes, untangling her thinking.

At the other end of her bedroom, the door opened. It was an abrupt opening. She looked up, startled. It was Rafe who stood there in the oblong of hall light. He was wearing his plaid wool dressing gown. His hair was smooth, as always. Julie's eyes fixed themselves on him. She felt herself stiffening in her chair.

He shut the door, quietly enough, and came forward to her over the white carpet. He stood in the alcove archway, at the edge of the heavy white-and-blue patterned portiere, and looked down at her. His hands were thrust into his dressing-gown pockets.

"I saw the light under your door." He turned and glanced around him, at the wide bed, turned open on one side, the pillows white under the bed lamp; at the whole big room with its bleached mahogany chests, its comfortable chairs, at the doors of the bathroom and dressing room beyond. "I used to live here?" he inquired.

"Yes."

He took a step forward into the alcove. His eyes on her face were sardonic. "You needn't be afraid of me," he assured her. "I haven't got any notions I shouldn't have." He surveyed the small room. The window was directly ahead of him. On his right, behind Julie, the wall was lined to the ceiling with books. On his left there were similar shelves, and in front of them another easy chair, bigger than Julie's, a footstool before it, another reading lamp and a table with a silver dish. He reached down and took the cover off the dish. It held his favourite mints. He put the cover back. He sat down in the chair.

"A perfect fit," he decided, and put his feet out across the stool. "This was mine?"

"Yes."

"What'd we do, sit here and read our lives away?"

"We spent a lot of time here, Rafe."

"Wasn't it dull?" His eyes mocked.

"I didn't think so."

"God," he said. Then, "Can I read?"

"Those are your books, behind you."

He got up. "My books," he repeated. He looked at the titles. He ran his hand across them. "The History of the Clans." "Legends of Iceland." "Bonnie Prince Charlie." "Who Wears the Tartan?" He turned. "Am I supposed to know what's in these books? I've read them?"

"You've talked to me a great deal about what's in many of them."

"I don't even know what a tartan is. I never heard the word."

"That dressing gown is made of a Stewart tartan—the Royal Stewart. You were interested from the beginning in learning about the Scottish houses. And there wasn't so much material on Iceland, but your father had told you some stories and you were always trying to find as much as you could about his country."

He pressed his fingers to his eyes. "I don't get it," he said in a low voice. "Do you?"

"I wish I did."

"Look," he said, and his eyes were cool on hers. "Tell me this. Were we in love, you and I?"

Julie could not answer.

He waited. Then, "So I guess we were. And we've been married fifteen years, you all tell me. I've seen the marriage paper. I tried out the signature. It looks exactly the same. So I've got a scar on my arm and a burn on my leg and a hole in my throat that Prescott says he recognizes, and my handwriting is Rafe Jonason's handwriting, and the baby looks so much like me, he scares me." He sat silent. He looked around restlessly. "Don't you smoke? I don't see any cigarettes."

Julie didn't say, "You don't smoke either." Instead she got up and went into the bedroom. She came back with an unopened box of cigarettes from a drawer, kept there for guests. She remembered and went back for a folder of matches and an ash tray.

He was watching her as she came back to him. His eyes went up and down the white robe. He took the cigarettes and opened the package expertly with a thumbnail. "You're a cute kid," he said. "That's quite an outfit, that white stuff. Makes you look quite a lot like an angel."

"Have you known many angels?"

"Huh!" he laughed. He lit the cigarette and drew in on it. She had never seen him smoke before. But only yesterday Edie had said, "He smoked when he was a boy, I don't care what Hugh thought. When he came here his fingers were brown with nicotine. I thought he was just pretending not to smoke in case Hugh wouldn't like it. But he never smoked after that. I know. The nicotine went away, and there were never any matches or ashes or cigarettes or tobacco anywhere around his clothes. I watched him for years."

He leaned back again and shut his eyes. Julie studied him. Something was dying in her heart; she mourned, but the dying went on and on.

He said, "If we were so much in love, and married all this time, why didn't we have kids sooner? Is this the first?"

After a moment Julie said gently, "Yes, he is the first."

"Just one of those things?"

"Just one of those things." If he didn't remember—

The thin spiral of smoke wove its way up through the warm air. He lifted his head suddenly and looked at her. "Well ... are you in love with me now?"

Julie said finally, "I don't know you now, Rafe. I don't know you."

"You've been married to me for fifteen years. If you loved me, you loved me. Or did you? Or can you turn love off and on like a faucet?"

Julie thought, it isn't a man's body you love, not alone his body, however dear it becomes; it's his spirit, his mind, his soul, his true being. Who is this man? What is his true being? Have I been deceived? This new person did not come from nowhere; this man who drinks and smokes but who has pretended not to, and who curses and says coarse and cruel and vulgar things. Have I been always deceived? Then I do not love. I do *not*. It is not the small vices that matter. It is the falsity.

Is he false?

He could have stolen, and I would have loved him and helped him pay the money back. He could have killed, and I would have stood with him in the dock and taken the death with him. There was nothing I would have condemned, nothing could have killed my love, if he had been a true man.

Is he false or is he deathly sick?

Rafe had been waiting for her answer. When it did not come, he shrugged, "Well, whatever it is," he said, "I don't blame you. I guess all this is rough going for you, too." He got up then and went to look at the books on the wall behind her. She had *The Golden Bough,* in its twelve volumes, and a lot of anthropology, and a good many books about Easter Island and Atlantis and Crete and Cambodia. They had been good books to read, when she was young. She knew a good deal about the Aztecs and the Incas, about the Angkor Wat and the Druids, the French caves and Tibet and all the safe things that were far away or long ago, things that she would never have to be close to. Rafe looked them over. "Don't tell me I've read these," he said.

"Some of them."

He moved back, bent and took up the top book of the three on her table. It was Morton Prince's *The Dissociation of a Personality.* He put it down again carefully and went back to his chair. He got another cigarette from the box and lit it. He gestured toward the book. "What's that?" he asked evenly.

Julie said just as evenly, "I've been trying to understand about you, Rafe."

"Getting anywhere?"

"I don't know." She considered. She said, "I know a man who's quite brilliant about these things. I went to see him the other day. He had a few ideas. I got these books from the library. It's a new field to me. I don't grasp the ideas very well."

He sat watching his hands. He looked at her again.

"What do you think is the matter with me?"

There was a tiny hint of helplessness about him. Some of the arrogance was gone; there was no real humility, but a lessening of the tough cold guardedness. Julie's heart warmed.

She smoothed the white nylon over her knees. "I don't know enough. But …"

"What's dissociation of personality? It sounds like what I've got."

"It's very complicated."

"What is it?"

"Well," Julie said, groping, "it seems to be … that is, some people … well, maybe it's like this. At some point in your life you get a shock. Something frightens you, or hurts you beyond bearing. So you can't bear to look at it and you shut it off in a corner of your mind. And then as life goes on, everything that happens that reminds you of that first thing gets shut into the same corner. If … for instance, if you had been terribly beaten when you were a child by your mother, that would be bad. Maybe not bad enough. Maybe if you saw your mother killed before your eyes by a … by a train," she said bravely, "maybe always after that the sight or sound or thought of a train would push whatever was connected with it deep into a dark corner of your mind. And all your thinking about trains would be warped and queer, and all your reactions to them not like those of other people. And gradually …"

"Well?"

"Well, so many things would get put away, painful things, sad things, bad things that had reminded you of that first terrible thing … they'd get all put away together, even words and phrases you didn't let yourself use in your real life, thoughts and tricks and ways, and there'd be a great mass of them built up. Linked together but not known to you in your real life. You see? And then …"

"Well?"

"I don't explain very well," Julie said miserably. "But if you got another shock, then the self you'd been living, so controlled and careful and good, would go under, maybe. Perhaps it would. And the other self, not your *self* at all, but this mass of hidden pain, would come to the top. All your inhibitions, fastened together, focused around some bad happening away back, something you don't remember."

He was listening. He said slowly, "Does that mean that the things you do remember ... maybe didn't happen? Maybe you just dreamed they might happen, maybe you ... just dreamed they *did* happen?"

"I don't know," Julie said, her heart yearning over him again. The shadows under his eyes were dark again. His whole face was shadowed. "Rafe ..."

"Well?"

"Would you like to talk to this man? He is a psychologist. He's very wise and kind."

"What would I talk to him about?"

"Anything. Everything." She leaned forward. "Don't draw away, darling. Listen. If you were to see him, Dr. Merrill, and tell him everything you can think of, every person, every place, every incident that comes to your mind, I know he could help you. We know who you are, darling, we know all about you. Whatever is troubling you didn't happen. It isn't true. We know you from the minute you were born. You have been here so long, and you were only a boy when you came. If you have some kind of horrible dream in your mind that frightens you ... you could tell him, and he could explain it away. I know he could. I know he could, Rafe."

Rafe sat looking at her. He finished his cigarette. For half a minute Julie thought she saw acceptance in his eyes. Then he got up in one swift movement. "You're a cute kid," he said. "Angel or no angel, you're cute." He reached down and ruffled her hair. "Thanks for all the advice. I'll go sleep on it. Maybe the old personality will do a double flop in the night and come up all slick and namby-pamby in the morning, the way you'd all like it." He laughed. "This guy Rafe you all talk about … maybe one of my troubles is, I hate his guts. He's too damned good to be true, and for me, I'm not having that kind of life. Not me."

CHAPTER TWELVE

JULIE GOT UP at seven o'clock and went through the corridor which led between her bathroom and her dressing room to little Hugh's nursery at the back corner of the house. He had been awake for some time, fifteen minutes or more, while she was washing and dressing. He was standing in his crib, holding a long involved conversation with himself. His face, when she went into the room, was a sudden huge smile, largely toothless but full of delight and love. "Mommy," he said in his lovely baby croon. "Mommy, mommy." He held out his arms.

He was soaking wet, from his neck to his toes. Julie lifted him out of the crib, holding him in two comparatively dry places under his arms, and laid him on his bath table. She stripped off the wet nightgown, the small shirt, the dripping diaper, and dropped them into the hamper. "I don't know how you *manage* it," she told him. "You're the wettingest baby that could ever be. You don't even get that much to drink every day." She poked his soft little tummy, flattening out now that his fattest baby days were over. "You mommy's boy today? Mommy's boy?"

"Mom-my," he agreed. He chortled with glee.

She had sponged him all over and rubbed him dry and was getting him into a dry shirt and diaper when Nellie came in from the other door. Julie smiled at her. "Go on back to bed for half an hour, Nellie. I'm up. I'll take him downstairs and give him his breakfast. I want to."

"Oh, I'm not a bit sleepy," Nellie said, her plump good-natured face relaxed and happy. "I'll clean up his room if you're going to take him down. But I'll be right along. I'm all dressed but my uniform."

Julie pulled on little Hugh's white wool dressing gown

and put on his rabbit slippers. She let him sit on her crooked arm, and they went down the back stairs together. Jennie was in the kitchen, with the kettle already boiling and tea in the brown pot.

"Oh, wonderful," Julie said. "Make enough for me, Jennie. Sometimes I wish we were English enough around here to take each other cups of tea in bed in the morning. It's a lovely idea."

"I'll bring you a cup of tea any morning you like, Miss Julie. All you have to do is say the word." She put a finger on Hugh's button of a nose. "I heard you, talking away up there," she told him. "I knew you were awake, my lad. An alarm clock, that's what you are, a regular old alarm clock."

"I don't see how he sleeps as long as he does," Julie said, putting the baby into his high chair. "I don't see why he doesn't drown long before he wakes."

"Boys are all like that," Jennie said. "I had five brothers and my mother said they was all alike. They're harder to train than girl babies, they wet the bed longer too. It don't make sense, except that men are always contrary."

"Pum," said young Hugh in a loud voice, pounding on the shelf on his highchair.

"Yes, pudding," Julie agreed, and went to the cupboard. She got down the Pablum and looked along the row of canned baby foods. She decided on peaches. She brought down a can, opened it, stirred the dry Pablum into it. Jennie had warmed the milk; she brought it over and poured it in while Julie stirred the concoction. "I'm cooking his bacon," Jennie said. "And making him a piece of toast." She patted the baby on his soft pale hair. "He's getting so *big*," she said wistfully.

Nellie came down as Hugh finished the Pablum. She said, "Miss Edie's in the living room, Mrs. Jonason. She's down early too."

"I'll take her a cup of tea," Julie decided. "You finish feeding this boy, will you, Nellie?"

Jennie handed her two cups of tea on the small tray and she went into the living room. Edie was there, her round face drawn and gray. She looked at Julie but said nothing. They sat down together on two chairs near the front windows, each with her tea, saying nothing.

There was nothing to say.

It was well, Julie thought, that Edie didn't know anything about her conversation with Rafe last night. Just as well.

He came down about half past eight, and they had breakfast together in the small room at the back of the dining room. He didn't eat very much. There wasn't much conversation. He looked drawn and gray too, as if he hadn't slept much.

What was the end to be, Julie thought? How was this to be resolved?

Edie said, "I'm going to church. Are you coming, Julie?"

"Yes, I think so." She buttered the last bite of her toast. She finished her coffee.

Rafe said, "Am I a churchgoer? I suppose I am a regular pillar of the church. I bet I am."

Edie got up abruptly and left the table. Rafe looked after her. His eyes, when they came back to Julie, were amused. "She's taking quite a beating over me," he said. "What'm I supposed to do about that? Is this her house or mine?"

"What do you mean?"

"Well, it's simple. If we get so we can't stand each other, which of us has to go, Edie or me?"

Julie looked at her nail polish carefully. She had always taken care of her hands, and they were good. The nails were long and almond-shaped. She knew she was vain about them, and she knew why. Perhaps it didn't matter. Perhaps nothing ...

"You haven't answered me, my dear little wife. You haven't answered me."

He was very handsome this morning, in the pale gray flannels, with his hair shining like pale gold and his skin scrubbed and clean. His eyes lifted at the corners in the old familiar way, and the lashes were thick and black. Very handsome. But her heart did not stir at sight of him. There had to be an end to pain some time. There had to be the death of the heart.

She said, "As a matter of fact, if you really want to know, the house is mine. So it would be for me to say, wouldn't it?"

He reached for the pewter coffee pot and filled his cup again. His eyebrows went up and down again. "Would it be at all possible that for all these years you've kept telling me about the house being yours, and the business being your father's, and me the poor orphan boy taken in on sufferance? You don't suppose I've tucked away all that and made myself a new personality out of it, do you?"

"It might be, Rafe." She kept her eyes down.

"I haven't even got a car, I discover," he said. "I went out to the garage yesterday and looked over the two standing there ... the black Packard coupé, that's Edie's, and the blue Buick, that's yours. I have no money in my wallet, I have no car."

"You had a car, Rafe. You bought a new one two months ago. You were driving it when you had your accident. It's a complete wreck. But whenever you want another, the insurance is ready for you. And you have plenty of money in the bank." She didn't want to say the words. She didn't want to tell him about the money. What might he do, this bitter, suspicious, angry man? What might he do?

"I see," he said. And then, with a flash of something almost like himself, a quick smile, he said, "I beg your pardon, Julie. I'm ... I keep forgetting ... I guess I'm a heel to you all," he said, and got up and left the table. In a few minutes she heard him leave the house.

She played with Hughie for a while when breakfast was over. She looked in on Edie, who was sitting in her room reading the Bible furiously, with the familiar spots of color high in her cheeks. She went on to her own room. She looked in the cupboard and decided to wear a black dress and the new powder-blue coat, full and soft, and the narrow band of blue velvet with a veil that made it into a hat, and black shoes and purse and gloves. She laid them all out and dressed carefully, getting her stocking seams exactly straight, brushing out her hair. It was getting very long; it hung almost to her shoulders again, and although she did not look her age, she was too old to wear her hair like a schoolgirl. She rubbed a little color into her cheeks, and as her fingers touched her left cheek she said again a little prayer of thankfulness that it was clear and clean, that the terrible stigma was gone. She said another prayer, under her breath; a thank-you to God that, in the days when the thing had been so hideous, she had had Rafe's love and tenderness....

But had she? Where, oh, where did the real man begin and end? How much of her life was real, how much of it had been false, false, the kisses like those of Judas, the tendernesses concealing bitterness, distaste, even contempt? Was it that her very ugliness had been the factor that had kept Rafe in iron control, that he had always been as sickened by it as had others, that he had played such a part of accepting it, of pretending to love her in spite of it, that he had been forced into breaking now?

She pulled on her gloves. She picked up the small soft suède purse. She looked perfect. She went to her door and stood there, leaning against it, her cheek pressed against it. She heard Edie bustle along the hall and go downstairs. She heard the clock strike the half-hour. It was half past ten. She heard the front door open and close, so perhaps Rafe had come in again.

She said to herself, I couldn't help having that terrible

thing. I couldn't. It wasn't my fault. Do I have to pay for it anyway? Dear God, do I have to pay for it *again?*

But it wasn't Rafe's fault either. It had nothing to do with him. It was nobody's fault.

So, of course, she *did* have to pay for it again, if there was any paying to be done. Again and again and again, to the end of her life. That was what responsibility meant. That was what it was to be grown up. If her thinking was even a little bit straight—if it had been the long tension of the hideous thing on her face, of her own fear of people, her timidity, her self-consciousness, her weakness, that had piled up the load that had finally broken Rafe—then it was hers to repair the damage.

Edie would never see that. Never

Julie thought, I'd better get along to church. I'm getting as confused as Rafe himself.

She opened her door and went along to the head of the wide staircase; she caught sight of herself in the hall mirror, a small person in nice clothes, not trying to look girlish but somehow, in the flowing soft coat and the blue band over her hair, looking about sixteen. She started down the stairs.

She was still thinking about her face. Without realizing what she was doing, she put her black-gloved hand up to her left cheek and went down the shadowy staircase that way. She realized afterward, when she had time to think it over, how she must have appeared to Rafe, who was standing just inside the front door, having just hung up his coat; as he caught a first sight of her. She must have looked exactly as she had looked when he first saw her, dressed in blue, eighteen years ago, with the black thing fixed miserably to her left cheek.

He looked up as she started down the stairs. She saw that he was there; and then, wildly, suddenly, he cried out, "Julie, Julie ... oh, darling, darling, no, no, no!" And like a flash he rushed up the stairs and caught her, and pulled the black gloved hand away from her face, and kissed her, and held her close against him, and when she tried to pull her face away from his she realized that her cheeks were wet with his tears.

CHAPTER THIRTEEN

AFTERWARD, WHEN EVERYTHING was over, Julie found that in retrospect she could remember every detail of that strange Sunday. It was almost as if, living through it, she were two people; one warm and loving and loved, living in a house full of relief and joy and gladness; meeting Rafe's return to himself, his overwhelming happiness in that return, the other cool, alert, watchful, even a little frightened. Definitely watchful.

Rafe was himself again. It was as if these past weeks had never been. His sight of her on the stairs had been the sudden shock that had, as Dr. Prescott had suggested might happen, "broken the bonds of memory" and let him be himself again. He had pulled Julie's hand away from her face, crying out to her, and then he had held her close in his arms as if he could not bear to let her go, and he had wept; and it was as if the storm were over and gone forever. Julie had cried too, and then Edie had come rushing out from the living room, had seen the new look on Rafe's face, his own look again, sweet and open and loving, and then after a few minutes she had led them both into the study, sat them down on the couch, shut the door and then sat herself down on a chair directly in front of Rafe, looking at him critically.

Rafe didn't pay much attention to her for a little. He was comforting Julie, drying her tears, patting her shoulder, running his hand down her arm, holding her close and murmuring to her. She began to get hold of herself. She pulled herself away a little and got her own handkerchief from her purse.

Edie, perched stiffly on her chair, her black coat open over her gray suit, her gray hat a little awry, said finally,

"Now, then, you two. Let's get this straight. What is this? Rafe, you look sensible again. Is that what's happened? Are you sensible?"

"If you call this sensible," Rafe said. He took Julie's free hand and tightened his own over it. "I feel as if I'd been away somewhere and just come back."

"Do you know what's been going on?"

"Yes. I think I do. Yes, I do. I had an accident, crashed the car, hurt my head. I was driving down from the cottage. I picked up a girl in Bracebridge ... Mabel somebody or other, she used to be a waitress at Echo Lodge ... and took her down to Barrie to turn her over to her husband there. You know, Julie—he was the boy who used to take care of the boats at the lodge, Bob, his name was. And I had waited for her to catch the bus, and that made me late, so I was driving fast. Too fast, maybe. Anyway, the last I remember there is that a couple of boys in an old car were coming north and one wheel was wobbling ... the thought crossed my mind that I ought to stop them because they were a menace to themselves and everybody else. There wasn't any way to stop them, so I remember deciding I'd stop at the next telephone and call the Barrie police...." He stopped. "That's the end of the chapter," he said.

"And what's the next chapter?" Edie demanded.

Rafe leaned forward and straightened the marcasite brooch at the throat of Edie's white blouse. He grinned at her, his old grin, warm and open and sweet. He said, "When do you take me to the woodshed?"

Edie began to relax. But she said inexorably, "What's the next chapter?"

Rafe leaned back. His arm was tight around Julie, his hand held hers with a strong, comforting grip. He said, "It's slightly mixed, my darling. It seems to be full of people I don't know, a tall man who looks like a houseman but isn't, a very possessive nurse with an unpleasant mind, and a general air of unfamiliarity about everyone.

120

Grimness, you might say." He said, "Wasn't I good, Edie? I feel a chill wind blowing from somewhere."

She said flatly, "You were the de'il himself, and I must say I still don't understand it. I'd swear that Auld Horny had got right into your soul, or pushed your soul out and climbed in himself. You were nasty, rude, vulgar, cruel, ignorant, selfish, bitter, vindictive, suspicious...."

Rafe put a hand up to his forehead. "I don't remember," he said under his breath. "I don't remember."

Julie sat up quickly. "Don't try, Rafe. Don't try, please. It's all over. Let's all forget it."

"No," Edie said. "We'll do no such thing. I don't believe in that wishy-washy way of doing things. The man that Rafe's been this past week is no creature of good. He's got to go, lock, stock, and barrel. And he's got to be dragged out into the light of day and look at himself. He was as hateful a creature as I've ever seen." She shifted on her chair. "He's got me half-frightened about myself, if you want to know," she said. "Is there another woman in me, hiding there underneath my church envelopes and my Christmas boxes for the poor, my sitting up all night with little Hughie when he's got the croup, losing my rightful sleep, my doing Jennie's work when she's got a lame back and pretending I liked it? Am I two women too, living in this creaky old body, with the other one just biding her chance to pop up and throw her weight about in the world?"

Rafe said slowly, "I was bad, Edie?"

"You were worse than bad."

Julie got up quickly. "Leave him alone, Edie. Please leave him alone."

"There, you see?" Edie said flatly. "The child's afraid too. She's as afraid as I am. Who are you, Rafe? Who are you, man?"

He had risen from the couch. He looked down at Edie. He bent and put both arms around her. He drew her to her

121

feet. Julie could not see her face; it was turned the other way, looking toward her father's fine portrait hanging on the wall, the wonderful painting by Cleeve Horne, the face strong and comforting and good and fine. Rafe held Edie. After a minute he said gently, "Forgive me, Edie. Forgive me."

She pulled away. She got out her handkerchief and blew her nose vigorously. She said in a muffled voice, "Well, if you put it that way, I've nothing more to say."

Nobody went to church.

It was an hour before Julie remembered to take off her coat and hat. She was dazed. Life was a strange, wonderful, mysterious, impossible, terrible thing. She felt as if she herself were dissociated: two Juliets living within one small, strained, tired body.

Edie did things about the midday dinner. Julie heard her in the kitchen, and once or twice, while Rafe was talking to Dr. Prescott on the telephone, to Mary Goodman, his secretary—telling her he would be at the office in the morning—Julie wandered out, lost and aimless, and observed what went on.

They had been planning to have a platter of cold ham, scalloped potatoes, a vegetable mold, and pudding. Jennie had mentioned these items to Julie earlier, as being simple and probably as wise as anything, since nobody was eating anyway—"the food comes right back out to the kitchen, a fair heartbreak." Jennie had said. But everything changed. Edie, rushing around with her hat on and her white hair poking out from under it in all directions, had dived head-first into the big freezer in the back pantry. She had come up with a leg of lamb, three boxes of frozen green peas, a raspberry pie, and a cellophane bag of green mint, picked and frozen at its freshest. She had had Jennie turn the oven on full, and she had run the sink full of boiling water, to immerse the lamb, wrapped in its plastic sheets, in the hot water. She was making mint sauce when Julie came to stand in the doorway, dropping the crumbled frozen mint into steaming vinegar, pungent and appetizing mixed with the brown sugar.

"Whipped potatoes," she was telling Jennie. "This is going to be a real dinner, Jennie. Mr. Rafe's well again, really well. Put lots of butter in them. Cream, too. Never mind the calories or the budget, my girl, nobody's eaten anything around here for a month, to be sure. Mr. Rafe's himself again, thank God, and it's a day to make the most of."

Julie went back to the study, and Rafe was there, sitting at the desk, talking to Robin. He smiled at her as she came in and put out a hand. She went to sit on the arm of his chair, and he pulled her face down and kissed her cheek.

"I don't know what it was, boy," he was saying to Robin. "I seem to have been a proper stinker. Edie says I was playing host to Old Nick himself. I don't remember. No. No, I don't remember. I don't remember anything from the time I saw that wobbling wheel on the old jalopy … and a while ago when I saw Julie coming downstairs."

He talked for quite a while, his arm close around Julie. Robin said quite a few things, apparently. It would be hard for him at the other end of the phone, Julie decided, not able to see Rafe. The voice was a little different, softer, warmer, more kindly. The words were different. She could envisage Robin as he listened, his kind face thoughtful, his eyes behind the horn-rimmed glasses concerned, his mouth firm, the fingers of one hand moving absently down the lapel of his jacket—probably a navy-blue jacket of fine worsted, this being Sunday. He and his mother had a pact about Sundays; he took her to church in the morning, very dutiful and trim, and then he went home and spent the rest of the day working on his book. He was doing a study of the criminal personality, giving case histories as he came upon them in his work as a lawyer. It would probably take him the rest of his life, but it would be deeply and sincerely written and would make a valuable contribution to human knowledge. Robin was true and fine and whole.

Sitting there beside Rafe as he talked, Julie looked up at her father's face in the painting. He had not been exactly handsome, with his long face, his square Scottish jaw, the thin lips lying evenly together, the level gray eyes, the high-bridged, jutting nose. But there was a look of great strength about him, of complete honesty and courage.

Rafe put the telephone back into its cradle. He turned to Julie and pulled her over into his arms. He bent and kissed her.

She struggled a little and got up, patting her hair into place.

"Don't go away, sweetheart."

"I'm not," she said quickly. She went across and sat on the sofa.

He followed her. "What is it, Julie?"

She looked at the knees of his gray flannels. She said honestly, "I don't feel as close as I might, not yet. I've been so worried, Rafe. Give me a little time."

He dropped down on the couch. He smoothed the hair back from her forehead. He said, "I guess this is what they call being out of your mind. I mean … I *was* out of my mind."

Julie thought yes, he was. But that's not the point. It wasn't his being out of his mind…. It was … it was … whose mind was he in? What was that other mind? What was it? What was it?

He was thinking with her. He said, "I don't understand either, Julie. You feel insecure, don't you?"

"The other person," Julie said with difficulty, "he wasn't a good person, Rafe. I don't want … I can't …"

"What does Prescott say? I mean, what did he say to you?"

"He didn't seem very worried. He thought this would happen. He thought you'd come back to yourself."

"Well, it's happened, sweet. It's happened. Let's rest in it."

She nodded.

"How much time have I lost?"

"Nearly a month. It's the twentieth of October."

"The twentieth!" He shut his eyes and shook his head. Then he opened them quickly and said, "The merger! It's all settled?"

"We didn't do anything about it."

He got up and stood looking down at her, his hands thrust into his trousers pockets in the old familiar way. "Why not?"

"The day of the meeting—well, I was ready to go down and sign the papers, Rafe. But that was the morning you ... you woke up. And you were so strange ..."

He went on looking at her. A cloud crept into his eyes. He frowned. He said, "And when I woke up ..."

"You looked at me," Julie said steadfastly, "and you said, 'Who the hell are you?' as if you'd never seen me before."

His eyes darkened. He turned and walked away from her, and after a long moment, back again. He said, "I was a stranger."

"Yes."

"If you had signed those papers ... you would have been signing away all your father's work, his holdings, his life's accomplishments, to the control of a stranger."

"Yes."

He nodded again. He said gently, "You are your father's daughter." He reached down and pulled her to her feet. "Where's that baby of ours?"

CHAPTER FOURTEEN

THE EVENING SERVICE in the small stone church above the hill began at seven-thirty, and Edie, Julie and Rafe, all a little tried after the emotional tensions of the long day, slipped into their pew just as the minister in his dark red gown walked in to take his place in the pulpit. He had a fine face, this Reverend Evan Lewis, the color of parchment, with straight, silvery hair lying back sideways over a high forehead. He was a Welshman, with a lovely voice; when he joined in the singing his clear, beautiful tenor often soared above the best tenors of the choir, effortless and pure, and obviously without any knowledge on the part of its owner that it was noted by anyone. He was a man of the spirit, Edie said, a man afraid of nothing, living in a world of the spirit.

Edie sat on the inside of the pew, Rafe next, handsome and correct in his black coat and striped trousers. There was no trace of carelessness in him now, not in his dress, his manner, his bearing. Sitting beside him, Julie found her mind floundering again in the morass of doubt and conjecture which had refused to vanish. This was Rafe. There was no doubt about it. This was Rafe. But …

Dr. Prescott had come to the house this afternoon, and he was completely happy about the recovery. He seemed to have no concern, no fears in his mind. He saw this thing as a purely physical matter; Rafe had had a blow on his head, his mind had got a bit mixed, he had recovered from the blow, the results of the injury had healed, and now he was himself again. It was as simple as that. Dr. Prescott was completely happy. "May as well admit," he said as he was leaving, "I wasn't pleased there for a few days, my boy. You got off on a wrong foot there somehow. But I've got a theory that whatever makes people dream, the part of the brain that functions in nightmares, gets uppermost in some of these cases. You sound as if you were living in a bad dream. We all knew that none of the things, places, people, you talked about were real. We all knew."

Rafe said lightly, "Did I say much?"

And Julie chimed in quickly, "Not much at all, darling. Don't think about it. It really wasn't anything to remember."

Rafe had given her a quick glance but had said nothing further.

Robin, coming in at tea time, hadn't been so easy. Robin had had a considerable shock. He wasn't satisfied about this thing, his manner said as he arrived. But he thawed a good deal as they sat around the living-room fire and drank their tea and ate some of Edie's best shortbread, brought out only on great occasions. It was with some difficulty that Julie kept him off the subject, got him to leave Rafe alone, to talk about his own book. Rafe helped her there. He had been interested from the beginning in this project of Robin's, the exploration of the special characteristics which go to make up a criminal, which set him apart from the rest of the human race. They had quarreled amicably about it for years, Rafe and Robin. Robin was sure that criminals were in a way subhuman, or in any case that there was something completely left out of them, and that if you knew exactly what that X was, you could deal much more intelligently with crime. Anyone could commit a crime in the heat of anger, in passion, in frustration, Robin thought; but the deliberate criminal, the man who gives himself deliberately to vicious deeds, has something especially wrong. He is not ill. He never was a whole man. His crime is pathological. He can't help himself. "It's as if he hadn't a soul," Robin had once said. And Rafe had answered lazily, "What is soul?"

The talk, the arguments, had gone on for years. So

that it had not taken long this afternoon for the two men to get on to the subject again. Rafe picked up where he had left off; but Robin had new preoccupations. Several times he was obviously on the point of asking Rafe personal questions, to try and get some insight into the sources of the personality they had seen manifested during the last ten days. At last Julie had got up, gone over to the other side of the room as if for a fresh ash tray for Robin, and behind Rafe's back had shaken her head.

That had startled Robin, too. It made him understand that she, too, had her doubts.

What were they?

Whatever they were, she was ashamed of them. This was Rafe, his own beloved self again, well and whole.

The congregation had sung the opening hymn, Mr. Lewis had prayed the opening prayer. The choir had finished a beautiful thing. "The marv'lous work behold amazed … the glorious work of heav'n…." The organist began to play "Jesu, Joy of Man's Desiring," and the four ushers went up to the collection plates from the flower-massed table below the pulpit and passed them through the church.

The Bach swelled up into the groined arches of the church. The stained glass of the windows glowed in the warm light from the high candelabra. People coughed a little, or rustled self-consciously, as they dropped their offerings into the green-baize-lined wooden plates.

Rafe turned abruptly and looked down at Julie. His eyes were startled.

But he was all right. In a moment he turned away again, and by the time the plates were returned to the table and Mr. Lewis, his prayer of gratitude finished, had begun on his sermon, Rafe had relaxed again.

The text was the thirty-fourth chapter of Ezekiel. Edie, on the other side of Rafe, opened her Bible and read it through with Mr. Lewis. It was not a familiar part of the Bible.

"Thus saith the Lord God unto the shepherds; Woe be to the shepherds of Israel that do feed themselves! should not the shepherds feed the flocks?

"Ye eat the fat, and ye clothe you with the wool, ye kill them that are fed: but ye feed not the flock.

"The diseased have ye not strengthened, neither have ye healed that which was sick, neither have ye bound up that which was broken, neither have ye brought again that which was driven away, neither have ye sought that which was lost; but with force and with cruelty have ye ruled them."

His clear sonorous voice went on and on. Julie was not listening with all her attention. Her mind was turning and twisting the parts of her own problem together. Edie was following the words in her own Bible with a gloved finger, her lips moving; but Rafe sat like a statue, his eyes fixed on the minister.

"Seemeth it a small thing unto you," Mr. Lewis read, "to have eaten up the good pasture, but ye must tread down with your feet the residue of your pastures? and to have drunk of the deep waters, but ye must foul the residue with your feet? And as for my flock, they eat that which ye have trodden with your feet; and they drink that which ye have fouled with your feet."

Rafe put his hand down abruptly and caught Julie's. She looked up at him, and his face was glistening with perspiration. He turned his eyes toward her, and they were glazed.

She caught at his elbow. "Rafe!" she said in an urgent whisper.

He was rising. She clung to his elbow. She turned toward the door of the church and he walked beside her, like a man walking in his sleep. They went through the vestibule and out into the blessed, sharp, October wind. Outside the door Rafe stopped. He sat down on the stone steps and dropped his head into his hands. He did not move.

Edie came out through the church door. "What is it?" she said sharply. "Is he sick again? What is it?"

Julie put a hand on his shoulder. "Rafe, darling ... Rafe?"

He lifted his head. He looked from her to Edie. He said in a low voice, "It's all right. Maybe it was hot in there."

"We'd better get home," Edie said. "Come on, you two. I'll drive. He shouldn't have come out, it's all been too much."

Back at the house, Rafe dropped into his own chair beside the living room fire and sat staring at it. The logs had burned all the way down and it was almost out. While he was there Henry Lake came in, his hands in white canvas gloves, carrying three fresh logs.

"Excuse me, madam," he murmured to Julie, and then went to lay the two small logs across the old fire and the big log over them. He did not look at Rafe, sunk in his own dark contemplation, but Rafe looked at him. It was a long look, a strange look.

Rafe had a brilliant mind. How had he known, in his confusion, in his lost thinking, that Henry Lake was not a houseman? There was no way he could possibly know ... unless he had a sixth sense ... unless he had seen Henry Lake in his policeman's uniform at some earlier time; unless he was darkly suspicious, as people are whose minds are ill, and expected a watch to be kept over him.

Was that it?

Suspicion—that was part of paranoia. Paranoids were dangerous. They could be terribly dangerous.

Did paranoia go with dissociation, with amnesia, with whatever else had been Rafe's trouble? Surely this was too much of a muddle. Too much.

Edie had gone to the kitchen. She came back with a pot of hot cocoa. Henry Lake held the swing door open for her and then passed through it himself. Edie poured out a cup for Julie, one for Rafe, and one for herself. "When you drink that, my lad, you'll be for bed," she said firmly. "This has been too exciting a day."

"Yes," Rafe said.

She sat down on the small sofa. "I should have liked to know what in the world Evan Lewis was going to make of that text," she said. "I'll ring him up in the morning and explain why we left, although of course he'll know, he's been here three times since you had your accident, Rafe. But I'd like to ask him why he chose such a text and what he was going to make of it. Probably a reminder that we've to pay for what we do. That bit about other people having to drink the waters we've fouled with our feet. It's not very nice, although the Lord knows it's done every minute. There's nothing remarkable about it." She set her cup into the saucer and looked at the fire. "Perhaps there's been something happened we haven't heard of," she decided. "Evan Lewis has both ears to the ground. Perhaps there's a new scandal about to break, and he was preparing the thinking of his flock. I've caught him at that a hundred times. In the morning I shall certainly ask him why he chose that text and what he said and why he said it." She got up. "You'll go to bed now, lad? You look fair worn to a frazzle."

Rafe got up obediently and put his cup on the mantel. "I'll go," he said without inflection. He turned to Julie hesitantly. She came at once and took his hand. They walked up the stairs together. At the door of the yellow room he paused. He said, "My things are all in here."

"Yes," Julie answered.

She went on to her own room. She undressed slowly and put on her nightgown and the white nylon robe over it. She turned the bed down. She went into the alcove, sat down in her chair, and waited. She felt miserable.

She sat there for a long time. She heard Edie come up to bed, and then, a bit later, Henry Lake. It was still only half past nine. There was no sound from Rafe, nothing at all. The door of her room did not open.

At ten o'clock she got up and went out into the hall. The door to the yellow room was shut. She stood and listened. There was no sound within. Half-frightened, she set her hand on the knob and turned it.

The light was on. Rafe was there. He lay across the bed, fully dressed, as if he had dropped there the moment he had come into the room. He was asleep.

She watched him for a long minute, but he did not move nor turn. His breathing was deep and slow. She got the eiderdown from the top of the cedar chest at the foot of the bed and laid it over him gently. She left the light burning, went out, and closed the door softly. She went into her own room with a sense of incredible relief, took off her robe, got into bed, and was instantly asleep.

She slept for hours. What wakened her, she did not know, but when she was awake she knew that something was moving downstairs, in the study under her bedroom. She lay silent, listening. The sound came again—not a cautious sound, not an identifiable sound.

She got up quickly, put on her robe, pushed her feet into her slippers, pushed back her hair. She opened her door noiselessly and looked out. The yellow room door was open; Rafe was no longer lying across his bed. The door of Henry Lake's room, directly across from hers, was open too; not more than an inch, and with darkness beyond it.

Rafe was downstairs, down in the study.

She crept down the long carpeted stair, not making a sound. The study door was open, and the light stretched out across the hall. As she reached the lower steps, a tiny movement in the living room caught her eye; and as her eyes followed it, she saw that Henry Lake was there, in his dressing gown, standing well back in the shadows. He had lifted his hand to signal her, to tell her of his presence. She dropped her hand from her throat. She nodded to him.

Rafe was sitting at her father's desk, under her father's

portrait. He was still wearing the dark coat and the striped trousers. He had a pile of books on the desk before him, and he was leafing one over with a hand that looked unsteady. He was making no attempt to be silent.

There was something else on the desk before him. Something unbelievable. He had a whiskey bottle, half-full, and a glass. As she watched him, her heart stunned, he poured the glass half-full of whiskey. He drank a good portion of it. He set the glass down with a thump.

She drew back quickly. She took three steps back up the stairs. Henry Lake moved a little forward. He shook his head at her. He motioned up the stairs. He pointed to himself. He would stay. He would stand guard.

CHAPTER FIFTEEN

At nine o'clock next morning, Rafe came down to breakfast. He looked wan and unrefreshed, but he gave no indication of having been up until somewhere near three o'clock, drinking alone in the study. Lying tensely in her bed, Julie had heard him climb the stairs at that time, heard him go into the yellow room and close the door behind him. Much later she crept to her door and listened, and then out into the hall to make sure that she really did hear Rafe's heavy breathing as he slept soddenly in his bed. The lights were out downstairs; Henry Lake's door was shut.

She bolted her door, took one of her sleeping pills—a rare indulgence—and slept for more than five hours. She did not hear little Hugh waken, nor Nellie tending him. She was dressed and downstairs when Rafe came down, and had had a minute to go into the study and make sure that there were no traces of Rafe's nocturnal pursuits. There was no whiskey bottle on the desk, no glass; the books he had been looking at were gone. Henry Lake had cleared away the evidence.

Rafe was quiet at the breakfast table, but except for that and his air of fatigue, quite himself. He said as he finished his coffee, "I think I'd like to try the office for a few hours."

Julie said gently, "Are you sure you're well enough, Rafe?"

"I think it might do me good." He gave her one of his warm sweet smiles. "You look done out yourself, sweetheart. Why don't you try to rest today?"

"I've nothing special to do," Julie replied.

"Well, I have," Edie said. "I have to go downtown. Rafe, would you like me to drive you? And, by the way, what are you going to do about a new car?"

Rafe said with a certain disinterest, "I suppose I'll need one."

"Well, of course you'll need one," Edie said. "Come along, dear, if you're really coming with me. I'm not sure you should go near the office, but if you stay only an hour or two perhaps, as you say, it will do you good. You had a long night's rest."

Julie went to the side door with them as they left. Edie bustled on out, to get into the driver's seat of her car, which Henry had backed out of the garage for her. Rafe stopped for a minute. He put his arms about Julie and held her close. He kissed her forehead. He said in an odd voice, "I love you, you know," and then followed Edie to her car. Edie wound down her window and called to Julie, "I'll tell Mary Goodman to keep an eye on him and pop him into a taxi if he gets the way he did last night. But he'll have his sea legs in no time, Juliet, so take that look off your face."

The car was gone, sliding out of the drive into Russell Hill Road. Julie watched it out of sight. She went back through the side hall into the big front hall and on into the study. She was standing there looking at the crowded book shelves when Henry Lake came in.

"Mrs. Jonason, there are a few things Dr. Merrill has asked me to do. I'd like to go about them while Mr. Jonason is out of the house."

"Yes, of course," Julie said wearily. Then, "I never knew him to drink before this accident. Never."

"He had about twelve ounces of whiskey last night. He holds it well."

Their eyes met. "Does that mean … is that … I mean, I couldn't drink twelve ounces of whiskey and not show it, could I?"

"It's a good deal, Mrs. Jonason."

"Do you think he's been drinking regularly? All this time, when we … I mean, there have been plenty of business trips. Many visits to Montreal and New York and

Chicago, even to London. He's flown the Atlantic several times. Before I ... before I had my operation I never went with him. Afterward, when I was well, I went everywhere for a time with him, and he never drank. But then there was a year when the baby was coming and when he was tiny that I didn't go at all ... and I haven't really started to travel with Rafe again because I don't leave the baby too much."

"He is not an alcoholic by any means, Mrs. Jonason. But it does not seem likely that he has been an abstainer."

She sat down on the red-leather armchair. "I'm confused, Henry."

"It is a very confusing business."

"What books was he looking through last night? Was he reading, or just ... filling in time while he drank?"

Henry crossed the room and ran his hand along the row of books near the floor, beside the fireplace. "These," he said. "He had them all on the desk, Mrs. Jonason."

She went to look. There were twelve or fifteen big books on that shelf; her father's doctor books, they had always called them. They were nearly all about diseases of the heart. Most of them were old and probably out of date. She read over the titles and got up, to look at Henry. "Does Rafe imagine he's got something the matter with his heart?" she asked incredulously.

"I was puzzled, too. He must have seen these many times. Has he shown previous interest?"

"Not very much. I think we all read them, or skipped through them, when my father died. He died of a heart attack, you know. He had angina, although he didn't know it. He thought he was as sound as a bell. But all his family dies of heart trouble ... all that are dead have died of that. They never die of anything else. That's why my father bought these books. He wasn't afraid, but he was interested."

"How old was he when he died, Mrs. Jonason?"

"He was only sixty. And strong and hearty … we had no idea, nobody had, that he'd a thing wrong with him."

"Did they do a post-mortem, by any chance?"

Julie stared at him. His thin young face was kindly, concerned. "Post-mortem? Oh, no! Why should they? He had all the symptoms of angina. The doctor in Huntsville examined him thoroughly and asked Rafe all sorts of questions. It's a very painful thing, angina, and the symptoms seem to be unmistakable. There wasn't any thought of a post-mortem, particularly with the family history. My father's older brother in Scotland had died of it only a few months previously. We'd had the news and all the details. My father's death was similar. It was terribly hard on Rafe. I'm sure Dr. Cornwall didn't even think of a post-mortem. Why should he?"

"If there was no doubt as to the cause of death there was no need," Henry Lake said. "Will you excuse me then, Mrs. Jonason? I'll make sure of being back by late afternoon."

Julie went upstairs, to sit in her own room for a long time, thinking. Or was it thinking, this confused turning over and over of vague, half-formed ideas?

Did Rafe think that he, too, had a heart condition? It was true that he had some Macrae blood. His grandmother had been Hugh Macrae's mother's cousin. The connection was remote, except that in the Highland clans there were frequently half a dozen ways of fastening in a blood connection. Had he discovered symptoms in himself which he had never mentioned, symptoms which perhaps he had observed in her father?

He had worked terribly hard since her father's death; the whole load of Macrae Enterprises had fallen on him then. He had never complained. True, he had been young and strong; too young, many had thought, for the responsibility, but he had taken it, and taken it remarkably well. His twelve years of training under her father's stern, con-

trolling hand, a heavy hand, perhaps, however friendly—
had given him fine training.

The drinking?

Julie put her head in her hand over that. The drinking, and the natural easy way he had smoked the other
night—as if both habits were part of his daily living.

There didn't seem to be any sound or sensible answer
to this confusion of identity, this complete contradiction
of personality.

She got up finally and made her way up the side stairs
to the third floor. There was no attic, as such, in the stone
house; but the end bedroom at the back had never been
properly finished and was used as a storeroom. It was fairly neat, because Edie cleaned it twice a year herself. But
it held a vast collection of treasure: old boxes of music,
pictures, two trunks of Julie's mother's special belongings,
a dress form which had once fitted Edie but now fitted
nobody, an old Hoover kept just to do the floors of this
room, skis, tennis rackets, a croquet set that had not been
used for a good thirty years. Hugh's baby crib was here,
his bassinet, his baby carriage. There was a great deal of
luggage.

She made her way along the end wall past that stack
of luggage. She thought she knew exactly what it was she
wanted; she was sure she remembered it. Once that cheap
brown case, supposed to be leather but probably nothing
more than colored heavy cardboard, had been to her a
thing of romance. She had seen it before she saw Rafe himself, seen the maid of those far-off days, the days of Rafe's
coming, carry the case upstairs and put it into the small
room Henry Lake had now. She had seen it several times
since it had been relegated to the top-floor storeroom.

It was there, standing neatly at the end of the row.
Probably it had never been used since its coming, not being of the character of the heavy leather luggage that her
father had believed in. It was obviously not used for dress

patterns or photographs, or Edie would not have left it here at the far end of the luggage pile. It was probably empty.

With her heart thumping, Julie bent and pulled the brown case out. It had few marks on it; a scratch or two, a patch of dust ground into one side. She laid it flat and opened it.

It was not quite empty. Two books were on the bottom, two school books, it appeared; a *High School English Grammar* and a small brown copy of Scott's *Kenilworth*. Both had Rafe's name in them. He had taken his two years of high school by correspondence, Julie knew; these books were almost new, not the dog-eared, chewed, battered, scribbled books of the usual school-boy. She leafed through the pages, and nothing was written on them. It did not seem that the grammar had been opened past page seventy.

The suitcase held nothing more. Or did it? There was the usual piece of material stretched along the inside back, with elastic along the top. Julie slid her hand inside it, and something was there; a letter. She drew it out, and as she did so her eye fell on the label glued there on the inside of the lid. "Pete's Luggage Shop, Prince Rupert, British Columbia."

The letter was from her father to Rafe. The sight of his familiar handwriting on the envelope brought a sudden pang to her heart. It was angular and thin, written with his own pen with its fine nib, the pen he always used. His name and the address of this house was in the upper left-hand corner, and a REGISTERED stamp was on the front of the envelope.

Julie drew out the enclosure. The paper unfolded with difficulty, not wanting to lie flat.

> My dear Rafe:
> I thank you for your note accepting my invitation

to come here to me. I feel sure that the trip to visit us will be enjoyable to you, and we are anxious indeed to make the acquaintance of Annie's boy. My poor Juliet, of whose affliction I have already informed you, has met few young people and I know you will be kind to her. I cannot quite tell you what sort of cousin you are to her, not being an expert in these matters, but I think you are her third cousin twice removed. The relationship is something of the sort, in any case.

I have registered this letter because, as you see, I am enclosing five hundred dollars in cash herein. I know that you have no bank nearer than Prince Rupert, which is still some considerable distance from you, and that you may need transportation there. I suggest that you buy as little as possible until you get to Vancouver. There you will need a complete outfit of new clothes. Buy good material, my boy, and good fit; cheap things are never an economy in the long run. Your clothes and your railway ticket will take a fair share of the money. Buy yourself a good wallet and tuck the remainder well into it. I remember you at seven as being a boy of open nature, fond of people, and forgive me if I warn you now that the sight of money in the hands of a young man in new clothes, whose lack of experience with the world might be quite obvious to the eyes of an unscrupulous person, might lead to difficulties which I should not like to have you experience. I suggest that you hold yourself aloof from strangers, male or female, until you become a little more worldly-wise.

Be assured, my boy, that we are looking forward to seeing you and will welcome you warmly.

Sincerely yours,

Hugh Macrae

Julie read the letter through again. She folded it into the envelope.

It was not a letter Rafe would have liked. Perhaps no eighteen-year-old would have liked it, money or no money. And a boy of that age, who had lived all his life with the rough older men of the woods, would probably have rebelled at the careful advice, at the suggestion that he could not take care of himself.

But he had taken care of himself. He had got here safely, and he had brought a good deal of the money with him.

She got up, the letter and the books in her hand. A sudden thought struck her. She opened the grammar again.

Rafe's handwriting had matured. This handwriting was the scrawl of an untutored child, formless and loose. Rafe's writing was very even, firm, controlled. It had changed a great deal. He *had* been young; her father had probably judged him by the writing on that earlier note. The handwriting of a child.

She carried the books downstairs, to her own room, and slid them into the top shelf, where they stood openly beside Rafe's other books. If he noticed them she would tell him that they had come from his old suitcase. There was nothing wrong about putting them there.

When she had put the books away she considered a further action. It was deeper treachery, it was disloyalty and spying. And it would result in nothing. But that was what she hoped, that it would result in nothing.

She got Rafe's keys from the drawer of his chest here in her bedroom. He had not thought to begin carrying them again; this first day of going to the office was not yet in his pattern. His car was gone, and he had not needed keys. Julie took up the ring: the car keys, recovered from the wreck, the office keys, the key to his safety deposit box at the bank, and the small key which opened the drawer of the desk in the study, already opened by Henry Lake in the search for fingerprints that would be authentically Rafe's. She took the keys downstairs and sat down at the desk, to open that locked drawer.

The silver pen box was there, and Rafe's bank book and checkbook. At the back of the drawer was a small stack of pocket notebooks, bound in leather, one of which he always carried for business notations. Beside the notebooks was a thick package of letters from herself, sent to him when he had been away on trips. He had kept every one. She took the package out and slipped off the elastic. They were in order; they were mostly old letters, dating back to the years when she had not been able to go with him. His trips had never lasted long; even when he flew to London he stayed only a week or so. These old letters had been sent to Montreal and New York, to Boston and Chicago and to Edmonton. She opened the one to Edmonton, written two years ago when Hughie was coming, and read it. It was as if it had not been her own letter, as if her whole point of view had changed. She had loved this man with all her heart, and she told him so in every line. But there was a kind of naïveté in the love, a simple childishness, a belief that he was interested in all her small feelings, her emotion over the baby's coming, her physical discomfort, even her diet and what the doctor said ...

Perhaps that hadn't been the way to write him. The letter was mostly about her. Perhaps she should have been writing more objectively, less selfishly, finding topics that meant more to him. But in her blind trust she had believed that nothing in the world meant so much to him as she did. He had told her so a thousand times; he begged for news.

She pushed the letter back in its envelope and fitted the elastic around the package. There was no need to read the others. She knew what was in them. Love and loneliness and all the small details of home, anxiety for his comfort, longing for the sight of him. Was that not possessiveness? Had hers been a demanding, a cloying love, the sort of love a man tired of?

And if he did tire of it, what would he do?

He had not lived a single life when it came to drinking. What had his life been otherwise?

She put the letters back in their place. She opened the bank book and the checkbook. She read over the entries one by one, but they were all familiar items. Taxes, car upkeep, tailor, church, doctor bills, the department-store charge account, club dues, cash for personal use—no large sums there, nothing strange.

She reached finally into the back of the drawer for the small business notebooks, a dozen or more of them three inches long and perhaps two wide. The writing was small, and much of it was abbreviated. Reminders to himself. The notebooks were dated. She took up one that was six years old; used the spring and summer before her father's death.

Robin's name leapt to her eye. "See Rob. S. re prop. warehouse." Well, that was clear enough. Macrae's had to have a new warehouse, and her father had his mind set on a piece of property out near Scarborough. Rafe had been going to talk it over with Robin. He had talked it over, and the two of them had gone to see it, Julie remembered, and thought the price was too high, with which her father had agreed.

Other familiar names lay on the page, and Julie went over them and the subjects they brought to mind. She had heard the business talked over every night of her life between her father and Rafe. She knew everything about it.

She had gone through a third of the book and was about to put it down as she had the letters, when she realized that new names were creeping in. She stopped reading to consider. She figured out the date of the last familiar entries and checked back in her mind. July, 1949. Well ... Rafe had made three or four trips to New York that summer; it had something to do with designs for kitchen furniture that Macrae's were thinking of. Rafe had been very careful about that furniture; it was a little bold, he had explained to her father, a little extreme, perhaps, for Canadian tastes. He thought he could get the designer to modify it just a little and make up a special line. He had talked about it quite a good deal, spent a lot of time on it, more than was justified, her father had suggested at one point. But Rafe was a perfectionist in many ways and he had persisted. The furniture had been a great success, although her father had not lived to know of the success. He had died that fall, in the first week of November.

These unfamiliar names … Retzky (that was the designer, wasn't it?) Norman, Carter … they would have been New York names.

Julie's finger went down the page with its small writing, its abbreviations. There were telephone numbers along the margins.

She turned one more page, her heart easy. She read, in Rafe's writing that was perfectly clear, "Send Chanel 5 to Beautiful."

Her eyes fixed themselves on the words.

"Send Chanel 5 to Beautiful."

CHAPTER SIXTEEN

WHEN RAFE CAME HOME in the late afternoon, Julie was sitting in the living room with the baby in her arms. She felt very calm. She looked up and said in an ordinary voice, "Did you have a good day, Rafe? Sure you're not over-tired?"

He bent to kiss her, and the baby reached for him with a joyful shout. He took little Hugh into his arms and held him high in the air. The baby chortled and shrieked, and Julie sat looking on and smiling. They made a pleasant homely picture, Rafe and the baby.

Nellie came for the baby, Rafe went upstairs to change into his lounging jacket, Edie came downstairs, and at seven o'clock they ate a dinner of cold lamb with hot tomato soup, currant jelly, baked yams and green peas and a fresh apple pie. Rafe looked a little tired, and he was quiet; he was thinking deeply about something. His remarks were only surface conversation.

Edie did not notice. She had something on her mind, too. She was going to the church immediately after dinner, to discuss a harvest home supper, the proceeds to be used for enlarging the Sunday-school room. She seemed to be completely satisfied about Rafe; as if his queerness during those few bad days had left her mind. Perhaps she had been able to accept Dr. Prescott's diagnosis; perhaps she really believed that an evil spirit has lived for a time in Rafe's heart but was somehow now exorcised, gone forever.

The coffee tray was taken into the study. Edie drank a cup hastily and then hurried out.

When she was gone Rafe's manner changed a little. He became even quieter. He settled himself in the red chair beyond the desk, drinking his coffee.

Julie leafed over the evening paper. She saw none of it, but she turned the pages carefully and slowly.

"Julie."

"Yes?"

"I know you so well. I know what's going on in your mind. I can't tell you how sorry I am."

She kept her eyes on the paper. She said in a low voice, "What is going on in my mind?"

"I've been thinking about it all day down at the office. I pretended to be paying attention to the reports I was reading over, but I was thinking about you. It's a terrible thing to hurt you, Julie. I wouldn't have done it for anything in the world, if I'd been in control."

She waited.

"Last night in church ... I suddenly saw what the queerness in my talking, in my ways, must have done to you. It was that business of ... fouling the waters that others had to drink. You are trying to live on something that you think is no longer pure and clean and clear. Aren't you, sweetheart? Aren't you?" He got up and set his cup on the desk. He came across to the sofa, and sat down beside her. "You've always been the soul of honor, of cleanness and innocence. And we've had a wonderful marriage, the most wonderful marriage in the world, built on trust and honesty."

She looked at him. His eyes were shadowed, his lips pressed together. He was searching her face, asking for something. For what? reassurance? An expression of trust in him?

"I love you very much," he said.

She folded the paper carefully. She said gently, "I don't think we ought to talk about these things until you are really well, Rafe. You look terribly tired."

"I won't be really well until we get them talked out. I can't live separated from you, Julie, I can't. You've been my ... my star and my anchor. I can't live without your loving me." He took her cold hand. "And you can't love me without believing in me, can you?"

"Maybe I don't know what love is, Rafe."

"You know, all right." He got up again and moved restlessly down the room. He turned. "Robin isn't my friend any more, either," he said. "I had lunch with him today. He watches me. I know how he feels. So I ... Julie, what really happened last night in church was that the two parts of my memory suddenly joined. I know everything now. Will you let me tell you? It's a long story. And I think I ought to tell Robin, too. I asked him to drop in about now. Is that all right with you?"

He looked very unhappy. Shut out, somehow. Julie's heart, dead in her breast, would not stir; but her mind said, he must be heard. Whatever it is he wants to tell me must be heard.

"Are you sure you want to tell us, Rafe? Quite sure?"

"Yes. It's a crazy story. Some people wouldn't believe it. But you and Robin will, after the exploring you've been doing. Oh, I don't blame you! There's too much at stake ... the merger alone is too serious a matter to put into the hands of someone you don't trust ... don't understand, maybe that's a kinder word."

"Rafe ..."

He came and touched her shoulder. "It's all right, darling. We have to clear all this up. As I say, I told Robin something of this at noon. And he suggested that he'd like me to tell the story to your psychologist friend, Jonathan Merrill, as well as to you and himself. And I agreed. After all ... it's crazy, but it's the truth."

Julie stared at him. Her whole thinking began to change, to lighten. Suspicion was a terrible thing. It was like a cloud over the whole being. Perhaps all the horrible things she had been guessing at this afternoon, after she had read the black notebook, perhaps they could be explained away too. If Rafe was willing to talk to Robin and to Jonathan Merrill, to let them hear his story, it must be true. And if there was an explanation for the strangeness that had gripped him then anything in the world could be explained.

There were footsteps on the veranda. "They're here," Rafe said. "I'll let them in."

Julie got up. She listened to the voices of the three men in the hall, Robin's steady and even, Rafe's quick and warm and bright, Jonathan Merrill's low and sparing. They came back into the study together. She held out her hand and took Jonathan Merrill's slim boneless fingers for a second. He gave her an absent smile and then looked immediately up at her father's portrait behind her. He did not mention it.

Rafe said, "Would Jennie have some more coffee, do you suppose?"

As if in answer, Henry Lake came into the room in his white coat. He looked at Julie. She said, "You are a mind reader, Henry. May we have coffee?"

He took the tray out, not glancing at Jonathan Merrill. Rafe did not seem to notice him. He was seating Dr. Merrill in the chair beside the fire, offering him cigarettes from the silver box on the mantel. He brought the box to Robin, who had seated himself in the arm chair near the door, near Julie. When the two cigarettes were burning, Rafe went back to the chair in front of the desk, with its back to the bookcases. He said, "My wife and Rob, here, have both told me that they have seen you, Dr. Merrill, in regard to my mental aberrations."

Something brushed against Julie's mind. When had she told Rafe that? Not since Sunday morning. Not since he had come to himself. Only when he was that other person—but she pushed away the thought. Suspicion was deadly. Suspicion had to be destroyed.

"Rather informal," Jonathan Merrill murmured. "Nothing very official."

At the word, Rafe glanced at him quickly, but as quickly away. Did he truly know who Jonathan Merrill was, psychological consultant to the police? Perhaps he didn't know. She had not told him. It seemed unlikely that Robin would have told him. But Dr. Merrill might not know this. He had used the word in all innocence. However, Rafe did not seem to be disturbed, as surely he would have been had he thought they had been in touch with the police. Jonathan Merrill had no police look about him.

Rafe said, "You teach at the university?"

"I do a few lectures there."

"I don't know much about psychology. I don't know the difference between psychology and psychiatry. I haven't much formal education," he said easily. "Is there a simple explanation of the difference?"

"It's a common question," Dr. Merrill answered slowly. "Both are comparatively new sciences. I suppose you could say that psychology is the study of the normal workings of the brain, the functioning of the various mental processes. Psychiatry, on the other hand, is something like the practice of medicine. It studies the mind in abnormality and then works at the correction of the abnormality."

"I see," Rafe said. "And you're a psychologist?"

"I am so classified in the university directory."

"So Julie and Robin, here, were really enquiring about me only as if I'd been normal."

"Concussion is common enough. Amnesia is not exactly common, although in very small doses perhaps it is commoner than we think. You were undergoing a fairly routine experience. It is never routine to friends and family, however. It is always very confusing and very disturbing to them."

The air was quieter. There was no tension in it.

Henry Lake came in with the coffee. He set the tray on the desk, filled the cups, and brought them round. He left the tray with its covered coffee pot on the desk beside Rafe. He went out. Rafe glanced after him quickly, but with no special concern. Perhaps he had been suspicious, too. Watchful, frightened. He did not know himself; he suspected everyone. Henry Lake did not quite fit in, and he didn't, somehow, look like a houseman. Was that all Rafe's remark yesterday had been, a natural wondering?

Rafe lifted his cup and swirled his coffee round and round in it. He looked at Robin, sitting unmoving in his chair. "Well," he said. "Here goes. I ... it was only last night that I got the hang of this bit; because what happened was that I suddenly realized the *reality* of the ... of the person I'd been from the moment I woke in hospital."

All three faces were turned toward him.

"I can remember now the whole thing," he said. "I can remember what I said and did, how I spoke, what my attitude was. It's all like a dream, but I can remember. I couldn't at first. Yesterday morning when I was suddenly myself again, suddenly Rafe Jonason, I lost that other personality. It was gone, forgotten, buried. Then in church ... I don't know why, I don't know what was said, or what chord the music struck, or what happened ... but I was suddenly the two men, that stranger as well as myself. And I know I've got to explain." He stopped. "It's really very simple."

Robin said evenly, "Go on, Rafe. It wasn't simple to us. It isn't simple now."

Rafe looked at him. "Don't doubt me, Rob. I've had a bad enough time today getting my own ideas sorted out."

"Sorry."

The log on the hearth cracked in two, and the pieces fell apart. Jonathan Merrill stirred in his chair. He set his coffee cup on the small table beside his chair and lit another cigarette.

Rafe sat turning his coffee cup in his hands. "I wish I knew some psychology. I don't. I don't know anything about minds. Or how they work. I don't think I ever paid much attention. I've just taken people whole, the way they seem to be. Maybe I've taken myself that way, too. I didn't realize ... you see," he said, straightening and putting the cup down, "what happened to me was that, for a while there, I'd somehow got into the mind of another person." He looked at Dr. Merrill. "Does that make any sense at all?"

"Can you be more explicit?"

"Maybe I'd better start back at the beginning." He took a long breath. "The beginning is ... well, I suppose it was my getting on the train at Vancouver, the day I started east. Maybe it was Robin's putting that word 'train' into my thinking that began to straighten me out." He stopped. "I was as ignorant as they come," he said. "You might have expected me to know something, living all my life in lumber camps. Men in lumber camps can be pretty rough. In a way I suppose I did know a good deal of life, but not as it applied to me. So I got on that train, raw and green, in my new clothes, with Hugh Macrae's money in my wallet— he'd sent me five hundred dollars and a letter telling me to be careful of strangers—which I certainly was ... anyway, I got on the train. I settled myself in the day coach, not having sense enough to get a sleeper. I was scared." He looked at Julie and smiled, his own charming smile. "I'd never been on a train, let alone a Pullman. I didn't know there was such a thing as a dining car. So I sat myself down there in the day coach, looking out the window. And I got a shock."

Robin bent forward and crushed out his cigarette. He clasped his hands under his chin and leaned forward, listening.

"Out there on the platform—it was morning, you know, bright daylight—I saw myself. Or a character so much like me that I really did get a shock. He was young and tall, and as fair as I am, and he had blue eyes and the same color skin. He didn't look afraid, though, as I must have. He looked at home in the world. I envied him. Maybe that was the beginning of the ... well, of this transfer."

"Transfer," Jonathan repeated. "Well ..."

"He wasn't very well dressed. He was carrying a heavy-looking club bag, shabby. His hat brim was a little too wide. He didn't have an overcoat. It looked as if he were planning to travel, but light." Rafe stopped. "He had a girl with him, and it didn't look as if she were coming along. She was hanging to his arm, looking up at him ... not very far up, because she was tall, too. And then the 'All aboard' was called, and they kissed each other as if they never expected to see each other again, and then he made a dash for the train. He came into my coach and bent over in the empty seat right ahead of me. He tapped on the window and said 'Bess!' as if she could hear. She came over to the window and tried to reach his hand against the glass, and then the train pulled out. And he stood looking at her as long as he could see her, and then turned and saw me. For a minute he just stared ... and then he grinned and said, 'Well, hello, brother! Where did you come from?'"

Jonathan Merrill crossed a knee carefully over the other leg. His eyes were on Rafe's face.

"It could be a long story," Rafe said. "I remember everything he told me. It must have made a tremendous impression ... almost as if I were listening to my own story. You see what I mean? I'd hardly known any boys my own age at all. And this one looked enough like me to be a twin. I've seen other men since who looked like me; we're not an uncommon breed, the blond Scandinavians. We looked alike, but we weren't alike, in experience, inside ourselves. I don't think he'd have talked to me at all if we hadn't looked so much alike. He was tough. He was lonely, too, because the girl he'd just left was his wife, and he didn't know when he'd see her again."

He gave Julie another swift, heart-warming smile. He went on with his story, and Julie could see it unfold. Rafe was meticulous in his detail. The two boys—the other was three years older—had spent the day together, getting off the train two or three times for sandwiches and coffee and pie. The stranger's name was Johnson. Alf Johnson, Rafe said; and they had found that queer too, because Rafe Jonason and Alf Johnson are not too dissimilar. He had been everywhere, this Alf. For the first few hours he had talked mostly of the places he'd seen and been to, and there were plenty of them. He'd been a cabin boy on a boat that went to China and India when he was fourteen. He'd tried riding the ranges of eastern Oregon before that. He talked adventure all day, with young Rafe's eyes popping. Then night came, and they got into the mountains and stood out between the cars catching the smell of the great hills in the spring. And then, after dark, the train had been stopped suddenly by a bad freight wreck on the track ahead … nobody killed, but fourteen boxcars of canned groceries had gone off the track and spilled open all over the rails. So they had got off the train to sit on a ledge of rock in the dark and quiet, waiting until the track should be cleared, and then Alf had opened up about his real feeling toward the world and the real truth of his life.

Rafe hesitated. "He was tough because he'd had to be," he said. "He'd got a bad start. He didn't know who his father was. His mother didn't know either. She was no good. Sometimes he'd lived with her and sometimes with her sluttish relatives, or in children's shelters, or just anywhere. Nobody cared anything about him. Nobody taught him anything. He scrabbled his way up, eating what he could get his hands on, wearing what came his way, sleeping anywhere that was handy. He was a complete outcast. He lied and stole and cheated, and although he had an idea that some people lived in other ways, he didn't know how. He lived as he could. And by the time he was in his teens he'd seen most of the bad things that can happen, and been mixed up in a good many of them—drink, women, a couple of sessions in a reform school." Rafe put a hand to his forehead in a weary gesture. "He told me everything in the world," he said. "And, at that moment, he was running from the police. He'd been in a waterfront fight with a sailor, and there'd been a knife mixed into the fight and he wasn't sure whether the sailor was dead or not. He'd got the fellow's duffel bag in the fracas down on the wharf and had got out of there in a hurry, back to the girl he'd been married to for three months. He was crazy about her," Rafe said. He stopped. "There'd been lots of other women in his life, because he had a way with him and women go for that ... but this girl had got under his skin. He was crazy about her."

Robin said evenly, "And this was Bess?"

Rafe stirred. "Yes, Bess. He talked about her all day and all night. Bess. He described her over and over ... and, of course, I'd seen her, there on the platform."

"She was tall and fair?"

"Yes, much his own type. He said she wasn't much good either, like himself. So he felt at home with her. He hated to leave her."

"Why didn't he take her?" Robin inquired. "Where was he going? What was he using for money?"

"Well, there was twenty dollars in money in a purse in the sailor's bag, and a ticket to Calgary, along with a couple of letters from the sailor's mother. He'd been going home to Calgary. Alf had a few dollars of his own, not much. But he and Bess decided he'd better get out of Vancouver. It would be too hot, if the sailor died. Alf would have preferred to go back to Portland, where he came from, because he knew the ropes around there, but Portland was the town he'd got himself a record in ... and so the ticket to the prairies looked just right. The idea was that he'd use the ticket to Calgary, find himself a job somewhere on the prairies—it might even have to be on a farm for a few months, because things were pretty tight out there in 1937—and when he could find his feet, he'd send for Bess."

Jonathan Merrill's eyes, fixed on Rafe, were pools of light. He had an understanding face; he was living this unhappy man's life with him as Rafe unfolded it.

Robin said slowly, "You never heard from him again?"

"Never."

"He wouldn't have been happy on the prairies. Nor his Bess. You'd have thought he'd have come on east. You'd have thought he might look you up some time."

Rafe looked at him and smiled. "I don't think so. He wanted to come east. He wanted money. But he wouldn't have looked me up, even if he'd known where to find me, and he didn't. Maybe you haven't had the experience of meeting a stranger and forming that deep intimacy … it's impossible with someone you know. It's nothing you want to renew. It's a relief to tell the story, but the person you've told it to is the last one you ever want to see again."

"Yes," Merrill said. "Quite true."

Julie moved. "What happened when you parted? What is the rest of the story, darling?"

"Well, that's all. When we got back on the train, about three in the morning, I went to sleep in my seat. He had settled himself across the aisle and I thought he was going to sleep too. The train started. When I woke in the morning he wasn't there. We had passed Calgary at day break. He surely got off there, as he had planned."

Jonathan Merrill said, "Have you thought about him frequently during the years?"

Rafe smiled at him. "No, I suppose that's it, isn't it? I've kept him separate, hidden, in a secret compartment in my mind. I've tried to … well, to be loyal to him, I suppose that's the way to put it. Loyalty is a big word. But there was something about his complete trust … you understand. I couldn't betray him."

Robin took off his glasses and polished them. His eyes behind them were larger than one would have expected, and often they had laughter in them which the glasses neatly concealed. Now there was no laughter. "Rafe, did you tell him your own story? It was romantic, too. Did you trade experiences?"

Rafe laughed. "No, I didn't, Robin. You have a very probing mind. No, I didn't tell. I was green and raw, and not given much to talking. Maybe I was shy. Maybe I was overcome with his superior adventures. But I kept thinking about Julie's father, who had written me a letter telling me not to talk. The letter made quite an impression on me. I was quite aware that it was Hugh Macrae's money I was carrying, and I kept hearing his voice in the back of my mind saying that I was to beware of strangers."

"Seems to me it would have been hard not to tell something," Robin said dryly. "He must have been a little curious about you."

"I suppose people like that are curious about everyone. But he was at a critical moment in his life, and wanted to talk about himself. All I had to tell him was that I was going East to visit my people, that they'd sent me a ticket. I wasn't a very interesting-looking person, except that physically I resembled him. He didn't really care anything about me, Robin. It was himself he was concerned with. I don't suppose he'd ever put his life together and told the story before. It was one of those times out of nowhere, if you know what I mean."

Julie said in a low voice, "I'm terribly sorry for him. No home, no love, no place in the world, no nothing. He must have been desperately lonely. No wonder he loved his Bess, even if she wasn't very good. Although maybe she was good … as good as she could be, if she'd had a life like his." She stopped. "I wonder what became of him, and of Bess? I wonder where they are?"

The clock in the hall struck nine. The room was silent. After a little Rafe turned to Jonathan Merrill. "Sir, do you think I have got this straight? I've been hearing myself talk during those first days out of hospital … tough, hard, angry. It sounds to me exactly the way this Johnson talked. I can't explain it any other way. It's as if I'd taken an impression of him at the time and somehow or other the

156

impression came up whole. Does that make sense?"

Robin turned toward Merrill too. He waited.

"It makes remarkable sense," Merrill said. "It is a perfect explanation."

CHAPTER SEVENTEEN

NOT MUCH LATER, Jonathan Merrill got up to go, and Robin with him. The air was clear, empty of tension. Rafe had lost his gray look; he was younger, freer, himself again. He stood with a hand on Robin's shoulder in the old way as they were all four grouped in the center of the room, finishing off the evening. Rafe had asked Dr. Merrill if there was any danger that this identification with the unhappy young man on the train, Alf Johnson, would ever occur again. It was extremely unlikely, Dr. Merrill had said. The airing of the story, the exposing of that troubling and engrossing personality, would exorcise it. He seemed to have no concern about the matter; his mind at rest. His clear eyes were remote again, as if his interest had been dissolved.

As they stood there in the big room, he looked up again at the portrait of Hugh Macrae. He murmured, "That's a fine piece of work. Was it painted long before he died?"

"Only a year," Rafe said. He dropped his arm from Robin's shoulder and caught Julie's hand. "We feel very fortunate in having it."

"There was a warning of his heart trouble?"

"No, none. But there was a long family history of heart trouble, and I must admit I was a little apprehensive," Rafe said honestly. "He was a very energetic person, very determined not to spare himself."

"You didn't say anything to me," Julie said.

"It wouldn't have been very good sense. But your father had it on his mind. The history went back for generations … all the Macraes died with their boots on, you might say; the heart just stopped. And when his older brother died I think he began to be really apprehensive … oh, not immediately apprehensive, not for himself. He wasn't afraid of dying. But he didn't want to die too soon. He wanted everything under control."

"And everything was under control?"

"It certainly was. He'd trained me to manage things ... a very careful training, exhaustive and strict. And he'd tied his property up very carefully for Julie, so that even if I suddenly sprung a leak, she would still have it in her hands."

Jonathan Merrill looked up at him, four inches taller, easy, completely in control again. "But he was sure of you? He'd made quite sure of you?"

"Very sure." He laughed. "He took no chances where Julie was concerned. Why ... you may call it undue caution, if you will. But on my first business trip alone, to Montreal, when he'd known me a good seven years, I discovered afterward that he'd had a private detective watching me." A muscle twitched in his cheek.

Julie said, "Oh, no, Rafe! Oh, my father would not have done that!"

"Darling, it's perfectly all right. I understood."

"But we'd been married four years ... he'd been so happy about you—he wouldn't have done that. He trusted you!"

Rafe said, "It wasn't mistrust, Julie. It was a sort of guardianship. We talked it out later, he and I. After all, I was still young. I was only twenty-five, and Montreal is quite a city. I didn't mind, even at the time. And later, we understood each other very well."

Merrill said, "What sort of heart disease did the family die of? What did he die of?"

Rafe's hand tightened on Julie's. It was Robin who answered. He said steadily, "It was angina, his first attack. He was only sixty, but if he'd had trouble we shouldn't have let him go hunting. Although I don't know how anyone could have stopped him, except that where Julie was concerned ... he would have given up anything if he'd thought it meant taking a chance of hurting her.

"It was a bad attack?"

"Very bad," Rafe answered. "I didn't understand at first. I thought it was indigestion. He had spasmodic cramps and violent nausea. I gave him soda, but it didn't help. Finally I decided he'd eaten something that had given him a touch of ptomaine, and I mixed up mustard and water. He was ill, then, and for a time seemed relieved. I thought a night's sleep would fix him. But he didn't sleep … the pain got worse, and …" he stopped.

"Cold," Dr. Merrill murmured. "Overexertion. He should not have gone hunting."

"Matter of fact, he was talking of giving it up," Robin said. "He knew what he ought to avoid. His brother in Scotland died while he was fishing, out in a boat on a cold day. He was going to stop hunting. This would likely have been his last trip."

"It wasn't only the hunting that took him north that time," Rafe said slowly. "He wanted to have a few days to talk things over with me. You'd think we had enough time together, but there were always interruptions. It was this whole program of the merger that was in his mind. He wanted us to turn it over and over, look at it from all angles, undisturbed. It was his idea. But as in everything else, he wanted to make sure that we were proceeding with the utmost care. I've tried to follow out his plans," Rafe said. "It's taken these six years to perfect them. Now they are all ready and we can go ahead."

Jonathan Merrill nodded. He turned to Robin.

"You must go?" Robin asked. "I'll drive you."

When they were gone, Rafe went back to his chair and sat down. Julie sank down on the edge of the couch. She said, "I have a great feeling of sympathy for the boy you told us about. I can see him. You made him so plain. You made everything so plain. I'm so *sorry* for him … the poor, poor child. I can see why you hid him away, darling. In a way I love you for it. You were protecting him."

"Don't give me any credit, Julie. I didn't know what I was doing. I'd forgotten him. I'd completely forgotten him. But as soon as I got that flash about him ... last night in church ... it all came clear. I wish I had talked about him now. I wish I had, sweet. I suppose he was my first big experience. I know now—I guess we all do—what a deep impression he made."

Julie traced a pattern with her fingertip on the red leather. "How on earth can people understand one another, truly understand? We carry such differences in our minds. Such strong memories, such vivid fears and dark confusion." She got up abruptly and closed the study door. She came back and stood on the rug before him. She said unhappily, "Rafe, darling ... I have a confession to make. I hope it won't hurt you. I realize now that in this house ... my father's awful anxiety for me, and his natural carefulness ... and you must have felt like a bug under a microscope. It must be a terrible feeling, belittling and bad. I ... I wouldn't tell you this except that I can't live except in honesty. Something curls up and dies inside me when there's deceit in me or around me."

Rafe said incredulously, "*You* have a confession to make? You can't have. You never did anything wrong in your life."

"Yes. It's ... about you. It's a nasty thing ... it's more of that old black thing, suspicion."

"You suspect me? You don't trust me, Julie?"

"Oh, I do now. I can see how wicked and wrong it is. The explanation for all your ... for all the things that frightened me is so clear. So I know that anything can have an explanation. And I know you'll give it to me. I'm ashamed of having the suspicion, but when it starts to grow it's like a bad weed."

"Is it something to do with this time of my illness? Something else I said, something you haven't told me? Or ... something about the business?"

"Neither."

"Well, then?"

"Well, today," Julie said miserably, "I went through the drawer in this desk, the one you keep locked."

He stared at her in astonishment. "But that's all right. Why shouldn't you? It isn't locked against *you*. It has my bankbooks in it, and your letters … nothing much else. I just don't leave it exposed to all comers, that's all."

"There are some notebooks in it too."

His eyes were steady. "Yes. Full of business."

"One of them says," Julie said steadily, "it says … send Chanel 5 to Beautiful."

Rafe got up. He walked over and poked the fire so that it sent up a shower of furious sparks. He came back. "I haven't the remotest idea what you are talking about. Not the remotest."

"It's written in the notebook. In your handwriting."

He shook his head. "Somebody's crazy."

"It was written when you were on a trip to New York. The spring before father died. There are a lot of telephone numbers, too." Julie said unhappily. "Oh, Rafe, Rafe … I'm sorry. I shouldn't have looked. I shouldn't have spied. And ever since I saw it I've been saying to myself … if he found a Beautiful, I'd have to understand. I'd *have* to. Because that was before I looked like a … before my face was fixed. And you'd been tied to me for years, ever since you were a child, really. I was anything but beautiful. I couldn't go anywhere with you. I wasn't a wife to show off with pride. And when you were away you must have been lonely. But … I don't know, darling, why the thought of your sending perfume to another woman … I guess it's just jealousy. It takes so much away from me. I don't know whether you understand. It makes a whole life apart from me … not just a momentary need for beauty, but everything else too. To meet a girl and find her lovely, to be shaken by her, to fall … that is a matter of terrible pain to me. But to be deliberate, to buy her presents, to do that with your conscious mind ... that is much, much worse. Because it is falseness. It is not what a true man could do." She stopped. "Forgive me, Rafe, forgive me. I know you didn't do it. I know there's a very simple explanation. But I've shown you what I think and feel. If you had done it, I couldn't love you; because I wouldn't know you. You would be a secret stranger, a deliberately deceitful stranger."

Rafe had been listening, his face intent. Now he took two steps and came to her. He set his arms around her. "You are an idealist," he said. "But I understand you. Julie ... you're quite right. The explanation is so simple that you can see why the whole thing meant nothing. You know who Beautiful is?"

Against his breast, Julie shook her head.

"Well, it took me a while to remember. She's Retzky's secretary. You know how important Retzky was to us. And she's a dragon, his guardian, practically. Without her you can't get anywhere with him. So I sent her a bottle of perfume big enough to drown in." He leaned away from her, lifted her chin and smiled down at her. "And she's as ugly as sin, with a hooked nose and a chin like a witch's, but smart as all get out, and everyone calls her Beautiful behind her back. Now. Does that make sense?"

Julie took a long deep breath. She nodded. She was faint with relief.

Rafe drew her over to the sofa and sat down beside her, his hand stroking her shoulder. The hand was warm through the thin gray silk. He said, "There ought to be some way a man could lay out his life day by day so that his wife would see and understand. It would save a lot of misery. Julie ... you must never doubt me. I could never love any woman but you. I could never, never turn to anyone but you. To me, you *are* beauty. You see? You always have been. Your eyes, your spirit, your sweetness, your generosity, your quick mind, the things you do for me ...

your beautiful baby … I couldn't even think about another woman. There is no one in the world I could think of but you—never was, never could be."

Julie slipped her arm around his waist. He put his cheek against her hair. They sat so together for long minutes.

The log in the fireplace broke again and a piece rolled out over the hearth. Rafe sprang up and went to lift it with the tongs and put it back. He brushed the sparks from the hearth. He turned back. He smiled at her. "It's been quite an evening," he said. "I liked your Dr. Merrill. Maybe I was a little resentful when you first said you'd been to see him, but I see why Robin had faith in him. He's sensitive and wise and understanding. I felt that he understood what I was getting at perfectly. Didn't you?"

"He is wise. He's not critical, or condemning. He just wants to understand. I can see why he is valuable to the police."

Rafe stood absolutely still. "To the police?"

"He's their official consultant," Julie explained. "I thought you knew. That's how Robin had got to know him and trust him."

"Robin? The police?"

"Heavens," Julie said, amused. "The police part of it had nothing to do with you, Rafe. Although … when you were so terribly different even Edie thought you were an imposter. We all did. I did. I knew it wasn't possible, but you were *not* the man we'd known. Not in any way. The body, but not the soul and spirit. Not even the content of the mind. That's why Constable Lake came to live in the house, not as police—only as Jonathan Merrill's assistant. Robin felt he had to bring that aspect in … but it was no police matter. It was just that Jonathan Merrill is so wise and so experienced in measuring people, and so understanding."

After a moment Rafe said, "I see."

"Rafe, don't be angry. Please. You *were* strange, oh so desperately strange!"

He said flatly, "I can see that. And, after all … I wasn't born here in this house. I *was* a stranger, in a way. Birth certificate, letters, mother's wedding ring, the remainder of your father's money … none of them were good enough. I was still a stranger."

"Maybe we are all strangers. Maybe that's why marriage is so important … when it's a good marriage, as ours has been. We're all lost and lonely, and if we can make an alliance that is open and true and sharing … as ours was—and will be again, now—we lose that feeling of being strangers."

He said in an odd tone, "I'm sure you're right." Then, "Julie … I think I want to go out for a walk. Do you mind? There's been such a lot of talk tonight. Or maybe I'd like to drive. It's raining a little. May I take your car?"

She went to him. The muscles in his face were tense. His mouth was set. She put her hands up and held his face gently. "You haven't had ten minutes alone for weeks," she said. "Of course, Rafe, go. I'll go up and read. I'd rather you'd walk, though, dear."

He said evenly, "You don't trust me to drive?"

"Rafe …"

He relented. He bent and kissed her lightly on the forehead. "I'm a nasty character," he said. "I'll let the night wind blow it all away. Promise."

He went. But he did not walk; he took her car. The spare keys were in a hidden place in the garage, in a small niche where a two-by-four had been sawed through and could be slipped out. He knew where they were. He got the car. She watched him back it out of the drive and swing it around in the familiar easy way, to head it east. At the corner he turned south, toward the city. He wasn't paying enough attention to where he was going. He should have turned north. He was heading straight for traffic and the frustration of the city streets.

CHAPTER EIGHTEEN

HENRY LAKE HAD LEFT the Macrae house by the back door a few minutes after Dr. Merrill and Mr. Robin Sloan had gone out at the front. He did not go out to the street but made his way to the back of the Macrae garden, to slip through the hedge at its corner and move along the neighbor's hedge to the side street. There was a car waiting for him there, its lights out, an impassive figure with a police cap reflected against the dim sky at the wheel. Henry Lake pushed his notebook further down into his pocket and got in.

"Hi," the driver commented. "Where you want to go, Hank? Merrill's? I've got your package."

"Yes, Merrill's," Constable Lake said thoughtfully. He glanced at his driver. This was P.C. Corson. He was a good man. Discreet.

"Some ways," Corson commented dryly, swinging the car out into the street, "some ways, you've got an easy job. It looks easy. No point duty, no patrol cars, no crawlin' up on deserted farmhouses waitin' for some lousy small-time crook to blast at you through the windows. No jail breaks." He turned into St. Clair. "But I bet you have a time keeping up with Merrill. I don't follow that guy. His mind don't work the way mine does."

"Yes," Henry Lake said. "I mean, no. No. It's a kind of basic mind."

"Hell, you even talk like him." He shot a quick glance at Henry. "You went to university, didn't you? We got a few others. Didn't you?"

"My father wanted me to be an historian," Henry Lake said apologetically.

"History? Dead stuff? Did you make it?"

"I got through the course. It gave me much background information."

"Yes," Corson agreed. "Well, it's a good thing you get along with Merrill the way you do. I'd go nuts." He swung the wheel expertly and the car turned south. "You got a case, up there at Macrae's? Or is Merrill just doing one of his research jobs?"

Henry Lake said slowly, "I don't know." He felt for his notebook. He had been sitting on the back stairs, just outside the back door of the study, taking down Rafe Jonason's story in shorthand. It was all there, in the notebook. "I'm not sure."

Corson went on down the hill. He turned the car into Prince Albert and stopped at Merrill's house. "Your parcel's in the back seat," he said.

Henry glanced along the street. Robin Sloan's car was not here yet. He opened the back door of the cruiser and lifted out the heavy, oblong parcel, wrapped in brown paper and tied with thick cord. "Thanks, Corson."

"OK.," Corson said calmly. "See you later, sometime or other."

Henry went up the walk, the string of the parcel cutting into his fingers. He was about to set the thing down and get out his keys when Jane Merrill opened the door. "Oh, Henry!" she said in surprise. "I thought you were Jon. He isn't back yet. What's that thing?"

He went in through the door she held open. He looked at her.

"Oh, I know," she said laughing. "I shouldn't have asked. Probably it's the atom bomb. You're getting more like Jonathan every day." She shut the door behind him. "Where is he? I thought he'd gone up to the Macrae house."

"Yes, he did. He was there." Henry went across to the far table and set the package carefully upon it. He took off his raincoat and went back to put it in the hall. "He left with Robin Sloan. He may have had something else on his mind." He stood for a moment looking at Jane. He had a sudden idea about what that something else might be.

"Well, come on over to the fire," Jane said crossly. "I get so tired of men with veils over their minds. I tell you what, Henry, it's turning me into a regular detective. I'm developing a system. After all, I've got normal curiosity, and I've had to be Jonathan's left hand often enough, heaven knows." She walked across the floor. She was wearing a pink sweater and a full swinging dark red skirt. She looked extremely nice. She took one of the chairs before the fire. "Come on, sit down and relax," she said.

Henry went across and took the other chair. He sat staring into the fire, his mind busy.

Jane picked up her knitting. She said casually, "What's she really like?"

Henry looked at her inquiringly.

"Mrs. Jonason, of course. Juliet Macrae. She's very pretty, I know that. Nice, too, people say. But what's she really like? She had a queer childhood, nobody can deny that. With that dreadful birthmark ... and all the money, and her father's terrific concern. Everybody knows that much of the story. What's she really like?"

Henry said slowly, "She's a lovely person. You would like her. You would like her very much." He considered. "I wish she had a friend just like you. There's nothing she needs so much."

"Well," Jane said. "My goodness, Henry, you're not being personal, are you? I mean, you haven't been sort of looking to see what I'm like, have you?"

He said seriously, "No, not exactly. No."

"I suppose you form conclusions by remote control. Well, never mind. Why does she need a friend like me? Why does she need a friend, period?" Then, when he did not answer, "What's she *like?*"

He thought it over. "Like brook water," he said, and was surprised.

Jane put her knitting down. She sat motionless.

"The only thing … all that will save her is her father's blood. He was a shrewd man. He was strong and careful and honest and shrewd. Most of the time, anyway. I don't mean to say that she hadn't got a backbone. She has. But she hasn't needed it yet. She's been cut off from the world."

"Is she going to need it now? Why can't she go on being cut off from the world?"

He said nothing.

Jane took up the yellow wool again. "Didn't this story the husband was going to tell tonight … didn't it hold water?"

"Oh, yes. Yes, it did."

"Don't you like him, Henry?"

Henry was puzzling about that in his own mind. At last, he said, "Perhaps I'm prejudiced. In those first few days, Miss Macrae talked to me a great deal. She was trying to find the answer to him. She rode her horse off in all directions, trying to find the answer. She told me at great length, in great detail, about his grandfather. It shouldn't have affected my judgement. I know better. I suppose I'd better get my mind straight on that one."

The floor-length gray linen curtains at the window beyond Henry fluttered suddenly. Jane glanced at them. She got up. "I opened that window," she said. "The air in this room is a perfect smog when Jonathan starts smoking." She went over to the window, the long casement reaching down to the floor, and pushed the curtains a little apart. She pulled the windows almost together and drew the curtains again, leaving a three-inch space for air. "Sometimes I think I'll have to take up smoking in self-defense. When you don't smoke, other people's tobacco gets down into your lungs and up into your head and in your throat and it chokes you." She came back to her chair. "Go on and smoke, Henry, I'll leave that window open."

He got out his cigarettes. He looked at Jane's slender pretty ankle and then firmly away.

"What were you getting your mind straight on?"

He lit the cigarette. He considered. "Probably he didn't have a chance," he said thoughtfully.

"The grandfather?"

He nodded. "I realize that there are psychopathic personalities. But your brother has taught me not to make snap judgements. They're rare. Villains are much more likely made than born."

"What'd he do, the grandfather?"

"Oh, the usual. Drank, beat his wife, exploited her, had a lot of other women. The usual picture of a man who's very insecure inside himself. He has to be a bully, picking on smaller and more helpless people because he's really extremely small himself. Usually he doesn't know it. If he finds it out, it makes things worse."

Jane nodded.

"When you see through such people you can't condemn them. You can't like them, but you have to understand."

Jane said, "*Tout comprendre, c'est tout pardonner.*"

"Not quite," Henry Lake said. "Anyway, that isn't the end of the quote."

She regarded him with some astonishment.

"At least, I don't think it is," he said. "Although, come to think of it, I have never checked. My French is not particularly good."

"What is the rest of the quotation?"

"Well … it changes the complexion. *Tout comprendre, c'est tout pardonner. Tout pardonner, c'est tout embêter.* To understand all is to forgive all … to forgive all is to bring everything down to the level of utter boredom—or, perhaps—to be asinine."

"I don't like that. It sounds smart. It sounds like Oscar Wilde. Somebody stuck that last bit on, some cynic."

Henry Lake looked at her thoughtfully. "Some day I will check. Not that it matters. Whether Mme de Staël said it that way or not isn't important."

"I hope she didn't. I liked it the way I knew it."

"I'm sorry."

"Oh, that's all right. It's something to think about. What you really said was that you could probably understand this grandfather of Rafe Jonason's."

There was a small sound somewhere outside. Jane stopped talking. She listened. She went back to her knitting. "I can't think where Jonathan has got to. He knew you were coming as soon as he left the house. When are you going to stop being a houseman, Henry?"

He got up and went to the front door. There was no one outside. He glanced at the partly opened curtain, ruffling slightly in the October night wind. There was an old lilac tree outside that window, its wood brittle and dry. The branches often rasped together. He came back and sat down.

"I imagine I'm about through," he said.

"You think this man Jonason is quite sane? He's all right? He isn't a reincarnation of the wicked grandfather?" She grinned at him. She had a dimple in the corner of her mouth. Henry Lake regarded it soberly.

"He is sane," he said. "He is quite sane."

"Does Jonathan think so?"

There were quick footsteps coming up the walk. Jonathan's key slipped into the lock and the door opened. Henry Lake got up. He felt a surge of relief. There were a good many questions that Jonathan Merrill was probably ready to take care of. It was time.

CHAPTER NINETEEN

ROBIN SLOAN CAME IN with Jonathan Merrill, his face stiff and pale. Henry glanced at him quickly. He was a good man, this Robin Sloan, a good man with a good mind, careful and anxious for the truth. He would have been as anxious for the truth, Henry knew, in any situation; his ties with the Macrae family, his devotion to Mrs. Jonason, had no effect on that particular anxiety. But these strong emotional ties were what made him pale now, gave his face the strained look.

Dr. Merrill laid his raincoat down carefully. He followed Robin Sloan into the room. He glanced at Henry. He turned to Sloan. He said, "My sister, Jane."

"How do you do," Jane said politely.

Robin Sloan looked at her, but he did not really see her. He came on into the room and shut the door behind him.

Jonathan Merrill stood for a moment looking at the open window, the gap in the curtain opening to the darkness outside. He turned and went to his own chair at the end of the big table. His back was toward that strip of cool darkness. His hand indicated a chair for Robin Sloan, who took it.

Jane said brightly, "Henry and I thought you were probably lost."

"No," her brother said. "Mr. Sloan and I were making a call. An old gentleman … a doctor. Dr. Cornwall. A few years ago he was supplying in Huntsville … taking the place of one of the doctors there who had the misfortune to break his leg."

Henry Lake looked curiously at Jonathan Merrill. There were more words than usual. He found himself a little puzzled.

Jane said, "It sounds very involved."

Robin Sloan spoke. He said heavily, "I don't find myself happy about any of this."

"No," Jonathan Merrill agreed.

"This man's daring, if that's what it is, is beyond all credence."

"Yes."

Jane said, "Do you want me to go, Jon?"

"No, it's quite all right."

Robin Sloan said in a low voice, "I blame myself. Macrae asked me to go on that hunting trip. There was something on his mind. I know that now. I knew it then. I misinterpreted. I think he had private information ... probably not final, probably not too serious. But he had suspicion. I think he wanted to watch Rafe, to test him. I think he wanted me to help. I didn't understand. I didn't go."

Henry Lake sat down slowly in his own chair. He pushed the big paper-wrapped parcel a little to one side.

"What probably happened," Robin Sloan said bitterly, "was that he faced Rafe right out with his questions. And they were true questions. Even if Rafe denied them ... he knew perfectly well that Hugh Macrae would not be fooled forever. As the rest of us have been."

"Not forever," Jonathan Merrill said gently.

"I could kill him. I could gladly kill him. It's bad enough for Julie. But for the baby ... for little Hugh ... for Julie, having that boy, this man's child ..."

Jane's startled eyes turned from him to her brother. She looked at Henry.

Sloan lifted his head. "You sat there and listened to him tonight. How did you know the truth? How did you know?"

After a moment Merrill said slowly, "The day you came here first. It seemed that there was one possibility we were all overlooking. It could have been that the man *was* Jonason, as it seemed, having lost his memory. It could

173

have been that the man *was not* Jonason, as you suspected, and playing a part, recently assumed. Or it could be that the man never had been Jonason. It was on this latest assumption that Henry tracked back to the critical point, back to the train trip east." He got up from his chair. He turned and went to the window behind him. He pushed the curtain further aside. He pushed the window farther open. He did not glance out. He came back and sat down.

"I cannot imagine anyone being so accomplished a liar."

"It's a talent that grows with use. After a time the truth is no longer any hurdle. When that time arrives, when there is no stumbling, no guilt, the story becomes very convincing. It takes effort, care, thought, in the early stages, but once the pattern of complete freedom has been established, complete self-vindication, the lying is almost not recognized as such. It becomes the truth to the liar." He moved a hand toward Henry. "Mr. Sloan will be interested in your findings."

Henry took up the scissors from the table before him and cut the string of the brown-paper parcel. The paper sprang back. He lifted it away, laid it carefully on the floor. What lay on the table was a bag, a man's club bag, shabby and worn. It had been carefully stored in a big locked room in a building owned by the railway company, a room in which reposed many other items of some mystery, items which some day might become important.

"Henry ..."

Henry Lake got out his notebook. He straightened himself on his chair. He turned on the green-shaded desk lamp. He looked down at his notes.

"I will condense, sir, since we have had the story already in considerable detail."

"Yes."

"This club bag was found in a sleeping compartment of the transcontinental train which left Vancouver on the morning of April 25th, 1937. It was found when the train was near the town of Maple Creek, Saskatchewan, about noon of April 27. You observe that the train had been delayed. I will explain in a moment. The passenger in that compartment had asked very specifically not to be disturbed, this at the time he took the compartment, in the early-morning hours of that day. This was understandable. The wreck had delayed the train for many hours. However, at noon the porter tried the door, thinking his passenger might have gone to lunch and wishing to make up the berth."

He glanced across at the pale, set face of Robin Sloan.

"Inside the compartment was the dead body of a young man. There was an empty whiskey bottle on the floor. The young man had drunk a great deal. His death had been caused, however, by a broken neck. He had obviously, or so the examining doctors concluded, staggered from his bed, fallen heavily, and cracked the back of his neck against the sharp edge of a projecting metal wastebasket fixed to the wall. There was a considerable conjecture as to how he could possibly have managed it, in the confined space; but the marks of the metal were on his neck, the neck was broken, and he was alone in his compartment. Also he must have been very drunk, or so it seemed."

Robin Sloan said, "You knew this tonight, Dr. Merrill, when you were listening to that story?"

"Henry brought in this report yesterday."

Henry Lake waited. He went on. "There was no prolonged inquiry. The dead man was nude, having apparently tried to prepare for bed, but his clothes were piled on the floor. His pockets held a few papers. There were other items in this bag. He was shown to be one Alfred Johnson, who had taken the train at Vancouver, although the compartment had been secured when the train started again, after the track was cleared, at a point between

Golden and Field. Sometime along toward morning, this young man had come to the sleeping car conductor and had bought a compartment to Toronto. He explained that he had spent the previous night sitting in the day coach, as well as the long hours waiting for the wreck to be cleared off the track. He had decided to take a compartment and sleep for at least a day. Other people on the train who had started out day coach, in that year of 1937 when money was still not easy, had come to similar conclusions and had asked for sleeping-car accommodations."

There was a long silence.

"What seems clear," Jonathan Merrill said at last, "is that the two young men met as we have heard. The conversation between them was not, I imagine, what we have heard. I should think that it was not the older one who talked, who related his adventures, told the story of his difficult life, so ensnaring to the imagination of the younger. No. That older boy, the man rather—for he was twenty-one—was not the sort who would have talked. It would have been the younger boy, the naïve lad from the woods, overcome with the wonder of the life that was opening up before him … remembering his mother's tales of riches and luxury, looking ahead, filled with the drama and excitement of his coming journey and the things that were to happen … it would have been he who talked, in spite of the warning Hugh Macrae had given. And in those long hours of intimacy, in the strangeness of finding at the beginning of his journey a fellow traveler in his own image …" He stopped. "I think he must be forgiven for talking," he said.

"They did, then, look so much alike?"

"The description of the dead man—boy—is that of a tall, fair, blue-eyed person, probably about eighteen. His papers belied his apparent physical age, but caused no great comment. The papers were accepted. He was married. His wife's name was Elizabeth Anderson."

Robin Sloan got up and went to the fire. He threw his cigarette into it. "She was found?"

"Not for some months. They sent the body back to Vancouver and the police tried to find her. They knew of the dead man; he was wanted. They had a dragnet out for him. They had no fingerprints, no positive identification. But the description and the possessions satisfied them. They had to bury him finally, but they had put notices in the personal columns of the papers. After some months Elizabeth Anderson came forward with an old clipping. Apparently she had mistrusted the notices, thinking they were an attempt to trace the man. When she did not hear from him she had to answer them. By that time this bag had been sent east; but in any case she did not want it. She had formed another alliance and the man was respectable. She wanted to marry him, but although her husband had vanished she did not dare. She came to the Vancouver police to see whether the Alfred Johnson, for whose relatives the newspapers had been inquiring, was her husband. She described him. She identified the pictures that had been taken of the dead body as those of her husband. He was not, of course, her husband, but the likeness was certainly pronounced, and pictures taken after death—particularly if one wants to be convinced—are not very satisfactory likenesses."

Jane said in a small voice, "Since you've let me stay, you can't mind my knowing this story. But I find it very confusing."

Robin Sloan, still standing beside the fire, looked down at Jane in her low chair. "I'll tell it," he said. "I'm trying to get it straight in my own mind." He stopped. "It's fairly simple, once you accept the fact that a man isn't who he has seemed to be for many years." He sat down on the velvet-seated walnut chair with its curved back, there beside the fire irons. His hand fingered the knob of the fire-shovel handle. He spoke, half to himself. "Rafe Jonason isn't Rafe Jonason. The real Rafe Jonason is dead; he was found dead on that train. Those are not his possessions, that bag and its contents; they belong to the other man, Alfred Johnson. His death looked like accident, but it was really ..." He stopped. He looked up. "Then we're left with this, to convince people that he *was* Alfred Johnson. How can you prove murder?" he demanded.

Jonathan Merrill said quietly, "I'm not sure we can. I doubt very much that we can."

"My God!"

Jane said, "Go on."

"I don't know how to go on, if we don't presuppose murder," Robin said. "It looks as if the two young men boarded the train more or less together, Alf Johnson being twenty-one and already a very hardened character. He got the younger boy's story. He knew the kid had money. He could see the glittering possibilities in his future ... and his own future was pretty grim. He'd not had much of a past, or rather he'd had a bitter past." He stopped again and, looking at Jane, recounted briefly the story of Alf Johnson's past, as told to the men by the man who *was* Alf Johnson, an hour or two ago. Jane listened, her face changing in sympathy with the facts of the story, the un-wanted child, unloved, uncared for, the hard growing-up years. Sloan finished, sat thinking, went on:

"You can see the temptation to change places. And it was not resisted. I don't see how you can postulate any-thing but murder," he said to Jonathan Merrill. "There was no point in changing places on a temporary basis. John-son could not have hoped to come east as Jonason and bluff his way—the other lad would have turned up sooner or later. He *had* to kill him!"

"Proof may be available," Merrill said mildly. "We haven't got so far yet."

Jane said, "Don't get ahead of me. How did the bad boy get into the good boy's skin?"

Sloan looked across at Henry Lake, who said carefully, "It looks as if he, Johnson, went up ahead and rented a compartment from the sleeping car conductor. It would have been simple. The younger lad, as we know from his true history and from the transferred memories of the man who talked tonight, the young lad would not have been able to do that himself. He wouldn't have known how, he would have been timid. So the older man did it. Then he came back and sent the young one up to the compartment with his own baggage."

Jonathan Merrill turned to Henry. "What was that baggage?"

"One brown suitcase, sir, and a raincoat. I have seen the suitcase. It is in the storeroom at the Macrae house. It has in it a letter from Hugh Macrae, the letter of which we were told tonight, cautioning the young lad not to talk to strangers. It has also two schoolbooks with the name Rafe Jonason written in them in a handwriting very dissimilar to that of the man who now calls himself Rafe Jonason. I suggest this is a point he has overlooked in spite of his great care, sir, or perhaps he felt that if any notice were ever taken of the differences in the handwriting, the early specimen would be put down to immaturity."

Merrill nodded.

Jane said, "How did the boy get very drunk? Do they know he was very drunk or did they just guess?"

Henry Lake remembered the report he had read so carefully. "The compartment smelled strongly of whiskey. The boy had certainly been drinking. There was no question of anything but accident, and the accident would have seemed practically impossible, no matter how rough the roadbed and how jerky the train, unless he lacked physical control."

"So what's the answer to that, Henry?"

"I suggest," Henry said seriously, "that the boy, the true Rafe Jonason, went to the compartment. He was a short time later followed by Johnson, who brought his own bag … this bag. He had whiskey in the bag. When he left, he took Jonason's bag and left his own….Everyone on the train was weary after the long enforced wait, weary, sleeping, not concerned about these two young men. As for the one who wished to get away, he could easily have left the train unnoticed at Calgary and gone to a number of places—any one of them—north to Edmonton, northeast to Saskatoon, southeast to Lethbridge—and from any of those cities he could have made his way to Toronto by varying routes."

Robin Sloan said, "The youngster had never done any drinking … or so we had always believed. But he would have seen plenty, in the lumber camps. Drinking to his future … with a new friend, almost a brother …" He stopped. "The man has great charm," he said. "He has always had great charm. It would have been so easy for him to convince the youngster that they ought to drink together. And perhaps to drink quickly … and drinks that were far too strong …" He took off his glasses, and his serious kind eyes were darkly troubled. He said, "I'm very much at sea. This strength, this terrible cleverness, this far-sighted planning, this ruthless disregard for others … to trick, betray, even to murder the young lad is something I can in a way understand. He would have been envious, bitter, because life was giving another boy, so much like himself, great opportunities. He would have been seizing his own. And he would have been discarding a dangerous past. I can understand that thinking, to a degree. But what about his wife? The girl he loved? Tonight. Rafe … well, Rafe spoke of her with great feeling. The man loved her, he said. He was speaking of himself. He loved her. But he could vanish from her life, leave her grieving, lonely, waiting … and go on to a new life with no concern for her."

"When we think of people being hard," Jonathan Merrill said gently, "we often forget what that means. We are all born vulnerable and anxious for love and acceptance. At first it is all self-love. The infant knows nothing but self-love. He has to be taught the other sort. He has to learn gratitude and tenderness toward others. That learning may never take place, either because there is no one toward whom gratitude and tenderness is due, or because the child is smothered with such overwhelming care and affection that he takes it for his inviolable right."

Jane said, "Hardness is natural? Selfishness is natural?"

"It would appear so," Merrill said thoughtfully. "The less mature the person is, the more selfish. And if the process of developing from love of self to the love of others never really begins, then it cannot develop, the individual cannot develop, and we have the completely immature man who is what we call hard, but who in reality is only absolutely natural, with the naturalness of the infant. Nothing can make him care for others; the equipment which he might have used for that caring has atrophied."

"That's damned clear," Robin said.

"And such people often acquire great charm which looks real. They do not understand love. But they see that sweetness and warmth in others brings results. So they mimic it. This man has been very successful."

There was a silence. Jonathan Merrill glanced behind him again, at that open window.

"When you came in," Jane said, "you seemed to be talking about another death that troubled you. Hugh Macrae's death. I'm extremely blank about that. Was that murder, too?"

CHAPTER TWENTY

HENRY LAKE SAID INTO the silence that followed Jane's question, "My mind is not clear on that point, sir."

Sloan said explosively, "Nor mine. I find myself sure and yet not sure. I don't know how it was done, if it was done, although if Hugh Macrae did have a weak heart … as Dr. Cornwall points out, they had been tracking through the woods, hunting; it was cold, bitter cold for November. They had got a deer, and Macrae insisted on carrying his share of the load for some miles back to the cabin. Rafe was very broken about the whole thing. There was no reason to suspect murder."

Merrill said, "Henry, will you tell Mr. Sloan of the discoveries you made regarding the seeming Mr. Rafe Jonason's past life … past, that is, in the sense of the time before Macrae's death, but after his coming to Toronto?"

Henry looked down at his book and turned the pages. He read: "At the time of searching Mr. Rafe Jonason's effects for a series of fingerprints which could be dated and identified, we opened with his keys the drawer in the desk in the study. Here we discovered a package of personal letters, letters from his wife. We found his bank books going back some years and checked the balances carefully, subsequently, with the proper authority, checking these various figures with those of the bank. We discovered an interesting fact in this respect. The accounts were in perfect order, but for many years the checks drawn to 'self' or 'cash' have been considerable, considering that all accounts, all costs of living, are paid by check. Expense account money was always lavish. Since at this time we had in our possession the key to Mr. Jonason's safety-deposit box, we procured a police order and opened it. In it we found some nine thousand dollars in currency." He looked up. "Mr. Jonason now has his keys, but he will not be given access to the box."

Sloan was frowning. "Did Hugh Macrae know of this money? It doesn't prove anything, anyway. It's suggestive. But it proves nothing. Is that what Macrae knew?"

Henry Lake went back to his reading. "At the back of the drawer we found a number of notebooks, obviously kept by Mr. Jonason over a period of years, ostensibly for business notations. Most of the entries pertain to business. But when all were sifted and examined, a considerable number were found—addresses, telephone numbers, even a name or two, a reference among the business items … which seemed to indicate what might be called an extracurricular life. We communicated with police in New York, Montreal, Chicago, Winnipeg, and various other cities, and there is much evidence to prove that the conjecture is correct."

Sloan said coldly, "This sort of thing was going on before Hugh Macrae died?"

'It has always gone on, sir," Henry Lake said briefly.

Sloan dropped his head into his hands. "Julie loves him. She thought he loved her. He told her so constantly. She has trusted him so deeply. The baby is his son."

"She is made of strong stuff, Mr. Sloan."

"Isn't there any way she can be protected? Isn't there any way she can be kept from knowing?"

"What do you suggest?"

The room was still again. After a moment Sloan said gropingly, "It isn't a police matter yet. You haven't actually put the thing into police hands."

"We have had much co-operation from them. They are not unaware that there are untoward matters in the background."

"You haven't any real proof of crime. You can't prove that this man murdered the boy on the train. You can't prove that he killed Hugh Macrae. If Macrae died of a heart attack through overexertion … even if he died of a heart attack after a violent quarrel in which he accused Rafe of immorality and of deceiving Julie … of living a double life … that isn't murder. You can't prove murder. The money in the deposit box can probably be explained. As far as that goes, you can't even prove that this man is *not* really Rafe Jonason. You can't prove it. What have you got to offer the police as a case against him?"

Jane said, "Did Macrae die of a heart attack? Don't you know?"

Jonathan Merrill looked suddenly very tired. He said slowly, "There are poisons which would kill, and after two days the evidence would be gone. But in any case, we can do nothing. The body was cremated."

Henry Lake made his final remark. "There are no fingerprints on the effects of the dead man in the train. None."

Sloan said bitterly, "So where are we? Where do we stand? This is nothing but a moral certainty, this guilt! We can't prove anything. If we could … it would break Julie's heart. She has had enough to bear, but this would destroy everything that is good and true and beautiful to her. If we can't … what happens? Does he go on living, this man … my God, he was my friend, my own friend … I loved him too. Does he go on with his masquerade, and all of us on guard, watching, trying to protect Julie, *knowing* him but unable to do nothing?"

The wind ruffled the curtain behind Jonathan Merrill. They were all watching his face, thoughtful, concerned, but oddly serene.

At last he said, "This is not yet in the hands of the police. No. But it is definitely a police matter, and in a few minutes I shall have to report it to Inspector Harper. I have no choice."

Henry Lake looked at him, suddenly surprised. It was

as if he were speaking to someone else; there was no one in the room but Jane and Robin Sloan and himself, Henry Lake.

"When the police get it," Jonathan Merrill said steadily, "they will begin to worry it. They will possibly not question the man at once, but they will watch him. Every move he makes will be watched. They will go back to the early days of the boy who was Rafe Jonason. They will go back into the life of the other man, Alfred Johnson. They will document the evidence of this present man's infidelities since his marriage. They will investigate minutely the death of Hugh Macrae; although it appears now that no one saw or heard anything that would suggest murder, this may not be true. People live in that north country, however unobtrusively, and they see and hear things. The thing is six years old." He stopped. "When you find a cancer in a human body you do not rest, medically speaking, until all the search has been finished and the cancer is rooted out—or the body destroyed."

Jane said slowly, "Suppose this man is innocent of all these charges. Oh ... not the infidelities. I suppose they can be proved. Of the two deaths. Suppose he is innocent after all. Suppose he did take the other boy's identity, and has been bluffing all these years, but is guilty of nothing more than that and the ... the betrayal of his wife. Bad as that is, bad as the whole picture is ... isn't there any way to save him, if he is not a murderer? Isn't there any way to ... to bring him to honesty, to save him, Jonathan? To make him a whole man?"

Sloan was looking at Jonathan Merrill too, his face a picture of doubt and fear, but with a faint hope in his eyes.

"The process would be painful for him," Merrill said slowly. "He would have to face himself, first, and see his own truth. Then he would have to face his wife, his friends; he would have to open up all his treachery. Has

185

he the courage? I doubt it very much. If he had the courage he would not be where he is today." He stopped. "He is a man in a strongly locked prison, the prison of himself. How can he get out? Remember John Donne: 'Mee thinkes I have the keyes to my prison in mine own hand, and no remedy presents itself so soon to my heart as mine own sword.'"

Sloan said slowly, "He would never look at his own sword, sir. He would never kill himself. That takes courage, too."

"Or desperation," Jonathan Merrill said quietly. "Desperation, the knowledge that he has no life before him, no freedom, no hope of freedom, if he is guilty. If he knew what we know about him now, I can imagine that he would take his car and drive ... he would not go far, perhaps to the Scarborough bluffs ... and send it flying over. Perhaps he has lived with fear for a long time. Perhaps this was what he was really trying to do, however unconsciously, when he had the other accident. Death is his only release. His burden is, if he is really guilty, truly insupportable."

They sat looking at one another, Jane and Robin Sloan and Henry Lake. Jonathan Merrill was staring at nothing, his eyes luminous. The air was strange, waiting. There was horror in it, an eeriness that Henry Lake had never before sensed. In her chair beside the fire, Jane shivered suddenly.

Merrill said, "If he were to come into this room now, this man, and say that he was no murderer; if he would tell us freely and openly which parts of the twisted story are true, if he would admit his other guilt, if he would help us ... we could save him. He would be a good man some day, if he would do this. It seems likely that even his wife, loving him as she does, with the gratitude she has for him, could forgive him and would help him. The cost to him would be great, but it would be worth it. We could save him. The police must have the evidence, the material we have collected. Society has its rights. But if the man is no murderer, he can be saved."

Sloan said, "I follow you, sir. But a *murderer* cannot be saved from justice."

"No."

There was a small sound outside the back window. It might have been the bare branches of the old lilac scraping together. It sounded more like a man's slow footsteps, uncaring, unknowing, lost.

The room was utterly still. Slowly, slowly, all four pairs of eyes turned to the door. They waited.

A sound came at the front of the house, the footsteps again. They paused. Then, after an eternity, they went on—down the walk, away from the house.

A little way down the street there was the sound of the slamming of a car door. An engine started; it raced, gathered power, the gears were engaged. The car drove away, faster and faster.

After a moment Jonathan Merrill got up slowly and shut the window that had stood open behind him. He drew the curtains. He said to Robin Sloan, "I must call the inspector, now. Perhaps you had better go home to be near your telephone. You will soon be needed, I should think. It is not far to Scarborough."